GUSS' GUTSY ADVENTURES

Published by

WS Education, an imprint of
World Scientific Publishing Co. Pte. Ltd.
5 Toh Tuck Link, Singapore 596224
USA office: 27 Warren Street, Suite 401-402, Hackensack, NJ 07601
UK office: 57 Shelton Street, Covent Garden, London WC2H 9HE

National Library Board, Singapore Cataloguing in Publication Data
Name(s): Yong, Germaine. | Bay, Alan, illustrator.
Title: Guss' gutsy adventures / written by Germaine Yong ; illustrated by Alan Bay.
Other Title(s): World of Science. Special issue.
Description: Singapore : WS Education, [2021] | "An augmented reality tale of a young bacteria
    navigating the human digestive system"--Title page verso.
Identifier(s): ISBN 978-981-12-4438-4 (hardcover) | 978-981-12-4541-1 (paperback) |
    978-981-12-4439-1 (ebook for institutions) | 978-981-12-4440-7 (ebook for individuals)
Subject(s): LCSH: Digestive organs--Juvenile literature. | Digestive organs--
    Comic books, strips, etc. | Gastrointestinal system--Juvenile literature. |
    Gastrointestinal system--Comic books, strips, etc. | Graphic novels.
Classification: DDC 612.3--dc23

British Library Cataloguing-in-Publication Data
A catalogue record for this book is available from the British Library.

Design by Alan Bay

Printed in Singapore

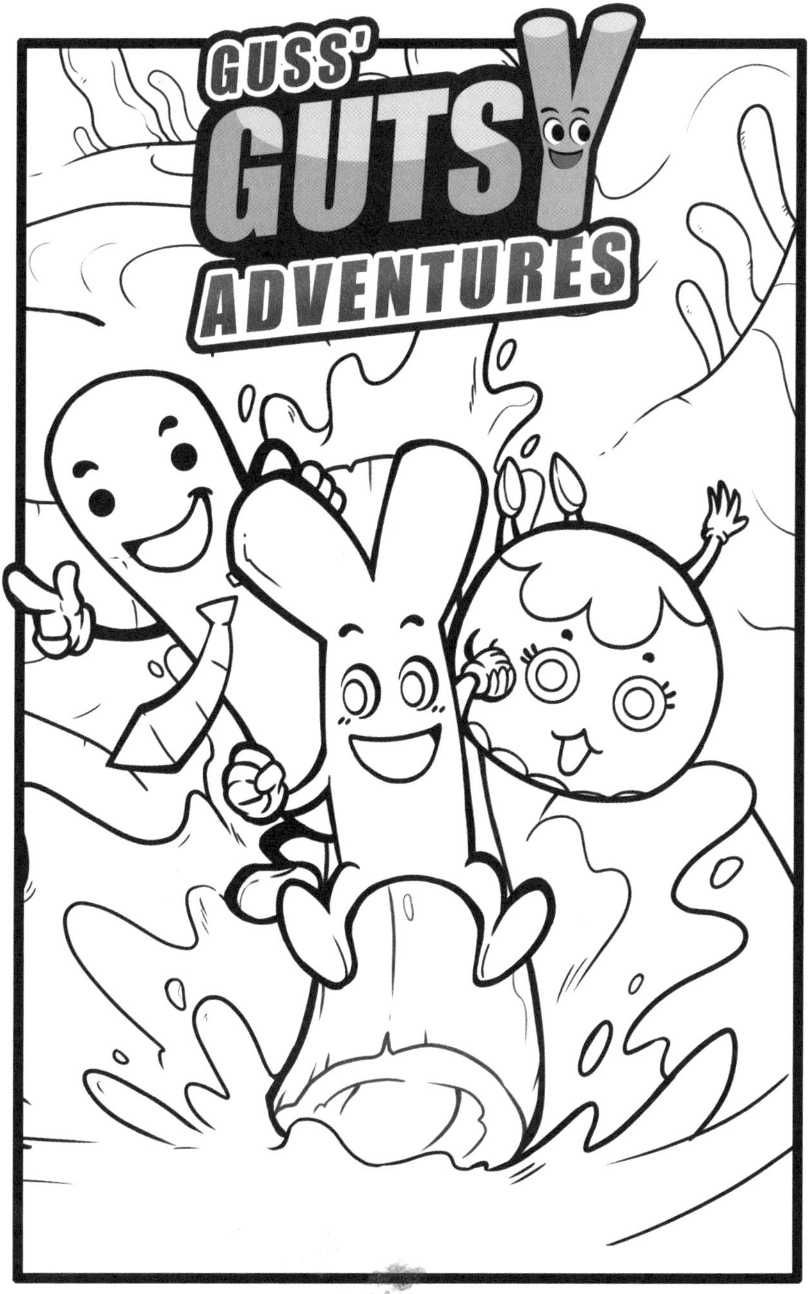
GUSS' GUTSY ADVENTURES

WRITTEN BY GERMAINE YONG ILLUSTRATED BY ALAN BAY

WS Education

NEW JERSEY • LONDON • SINGAPORE • BEIJING • SHANGHAI • HONG KONG • TAIPEI • CHENNAI • TOKYO

A Guide to Experiencing Augmented Reality in This Book

1

SnapLearn

Download the SnapLearn app.

2

Scan

Activate by scanning this book's barcode. Then, tap on the book cover image on your screen.

3

AR

Wherever you see this icon, scan the whole page.

Download on the App Store | GET IT ON Google Play

SnapLearn is compatible with devices running minimally on iOS 8 and Android 5.0 with gyroscope. For the best AR experience, please scan the physical or PDF version of the book. For any app-related issues, please contact us via email at hello@snaplearn.com.

Powered By : SnapLearn

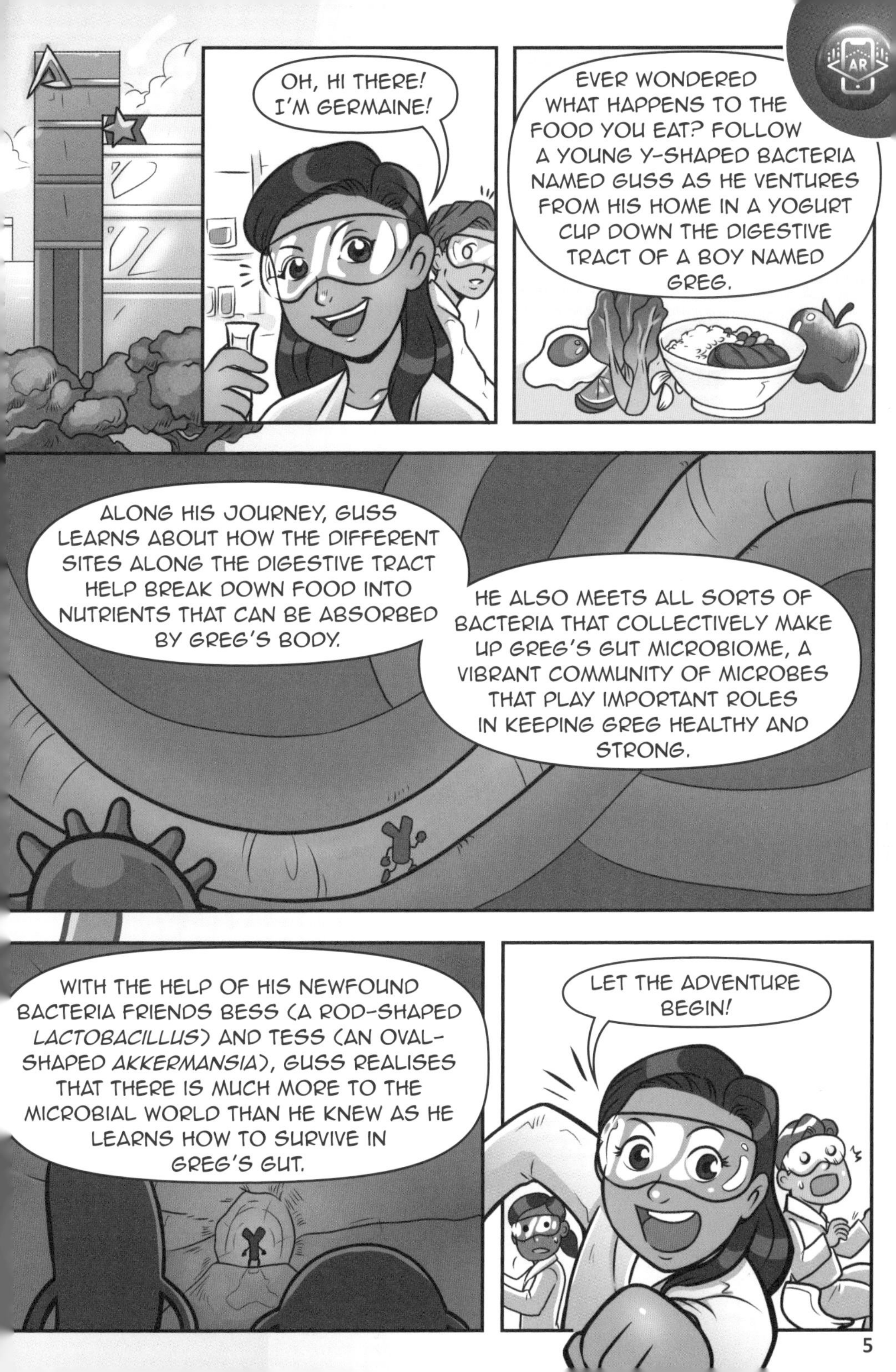
OH, HI THERE! I'M GERMAINE!
EVER WONDERED WHAT HAPPENS TO THE FOOD YOU EAT? FOLLOW A YOUNG Y-SHAPED BACTERIA NAMED GUSS AS HE VENTURES FROM HIS HOME IN A YOGURT CUP DOWN THE DIGESTIVE TRACT OF A BOY NAMED GREG.
ALONG HIS JOURNEY, GUSS LEARNS ABOUT HOW THE DIFFERENT SITES ALONG THE DIGESTIVE TRACT HELP BREAK DOWN FOOD INTO NUTRIENTS THAT CAN BE ABSORBED BY GREG'S BODY.
HE ALSO MEETS ALL SORTS OF BACTERIA THAT COLLECTIVELY MAKE UP GREG'S GUT MICROBIOME, A VIBRANT COMMUNITY OF MICROBES THAT PLAY IMPORTANT ROLES IN KEEPING GREG HEALTHY AND STRONG.
WITH THE HELP OF HIS NEWFOUND BACTERIA FRIENDS BESS (A ROD-SHAPED *LACTOBACILLUS*) AND TESS (AN OVAL-SHAPED *AKKERMANSIA*), GUSS REALISES THAT THERE IS MUCH MORE TO THE MICROBIAL WORLD THAN HE KNEW AS HE LEARNS HOW TO SURVIVE IN GREG'S GUT.
LET THE ADVENTURE BEGIN!
AR

Bacteria are tiny single-celled microorganisms that are invisible to the naked eye. They were among the first life forms to appear on Earth and are present in most habitats, including in and on the human body where they play essential roles in keeping us healthy.

Bacteria are prokaryotes, meaning that unlike eukaryotes such as humans, they lack a defined nucleus to organise their DNA and often have only a single chromosome. Bacteria exist in a variety of shapes, ranging from spheres to rods and spirals. Many bacteria that live in the human gut are adapted to living without oxygen.
Here are more unique facts about the story's three main characters:

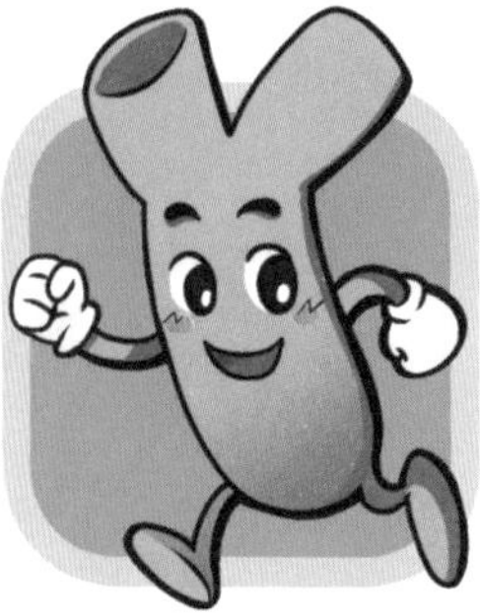

Guss is a Y-shaped *Bifidobacterium*. He is an excellent producer of short-chain fatty acids, which act as nutrients and as signalling molecules to keep our gut and body healthy. *Bifidobacteria* like Guss play critical roles in keeping babies healthy. Given their roles in promoting health, *Bifidobacteria* are commonly found in probiotics, which are foods and supplements that help to improve gut health.

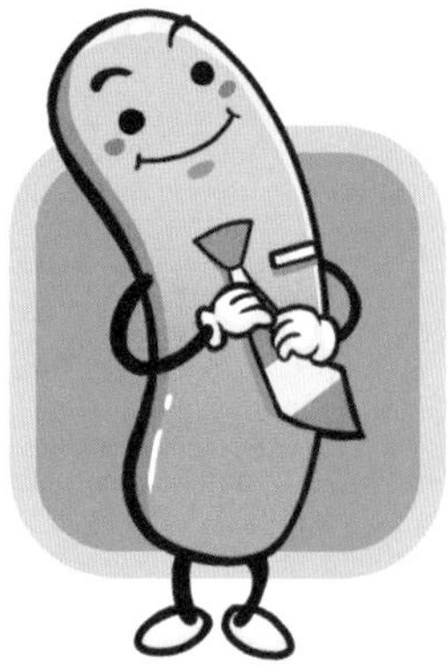

Bess is a rod-shaped *Lactobacillus*. *Lactobacilli* are good bacteria normally found in our digestive and urinary systems without causing disease. *Lactobacilli* produce lactic acid and often contribute to the sour taste found in fermented foods like yogurt and kimchi. Similar to *Bifidobacteria*, *Lactobacilli* are also commonly found in probiotics and prescribed by doctors to patients suffering from diarrhoea.

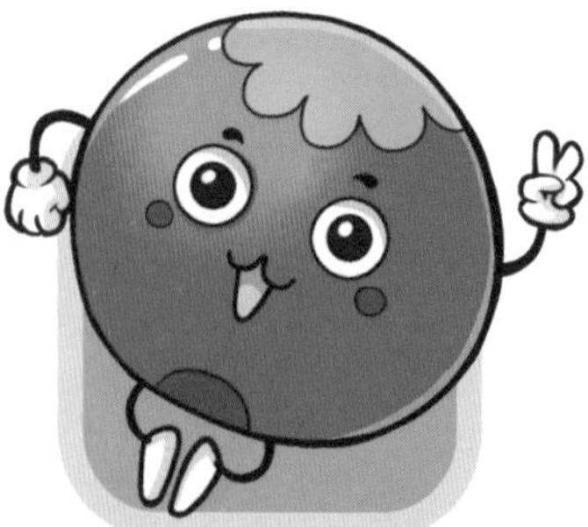

Tess is an oval-shaped *Akkermansia*. *Akkermansia* bacteria were only discovered relatively recently in 2004 by Dutch scientists. They are very good at breaking down mucus in the gut for food, and have been actively studied to better understand how they regulate metabolism in humans. Interestingly, they have only been found in humans who live in more industrialised societies, and are missing in the guts of humans that live isolated, agrarian lifestyles.

HELLO! I'M GUSS, YOUR FRIENDLY NEIGHBOURHOOD BACTERIUM. I'M A *BIFIDOBACTERIUM*, WHICH IS WHY I'M SHAPED LIKE A Y. I LOVE HANGING OUT WITH MY FAMILY AND FRIENDS.

GREG, REMEMBER TO EAT YOUR YOGURT!

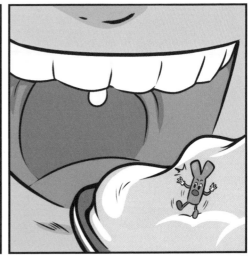

WHAT'S GOING ON?? WHY IS IT SO DARK AND WARM IN HERE? LET ME FIND A PLACE TO REST.

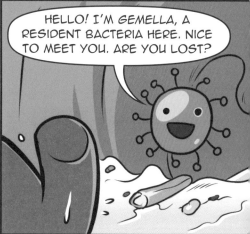

HELLO! I'M GEMELLA, A RESIDENT BACTERIA HERE. NICE TO MEET YOU. ARE YOU LOST?

YES, I THINK I'M LOST! WHERE AM I?

THIS IS GREG'S MOUTH. YOU'RE SITTING ON HIS TONGUE.

HANG ON TIGHT, I THINK HE IS ABOUT TO SWALLOW.

Parts of our mouth

Teeth: help chew food into smaller pieces before swallowing.

Gums: keep teeth in place and protect our body against bad bacteria.

Salivary glands in cheek: produce digestive enzymes that help break down food, in particular amylase which breaks down starch.

Soft palate and uvula: prevent food and liquids from travelling up to the nose.

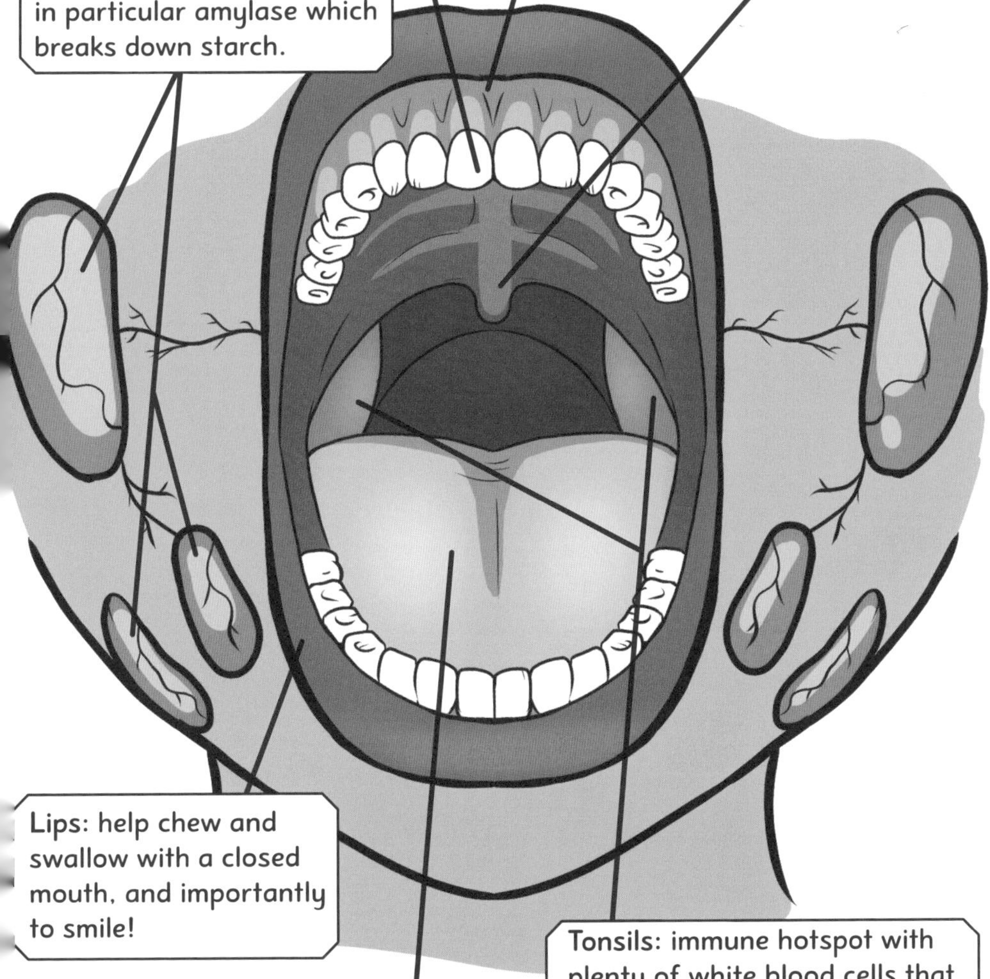

Lips: help chew and swallow with a closed mouth, and importantly to smile!

Tongue: helps with swallowing food, speech and taste.

Tonsils: immune hotspot with plenty of white blood cells that prevent germs from entering the body through the mouth and nose.

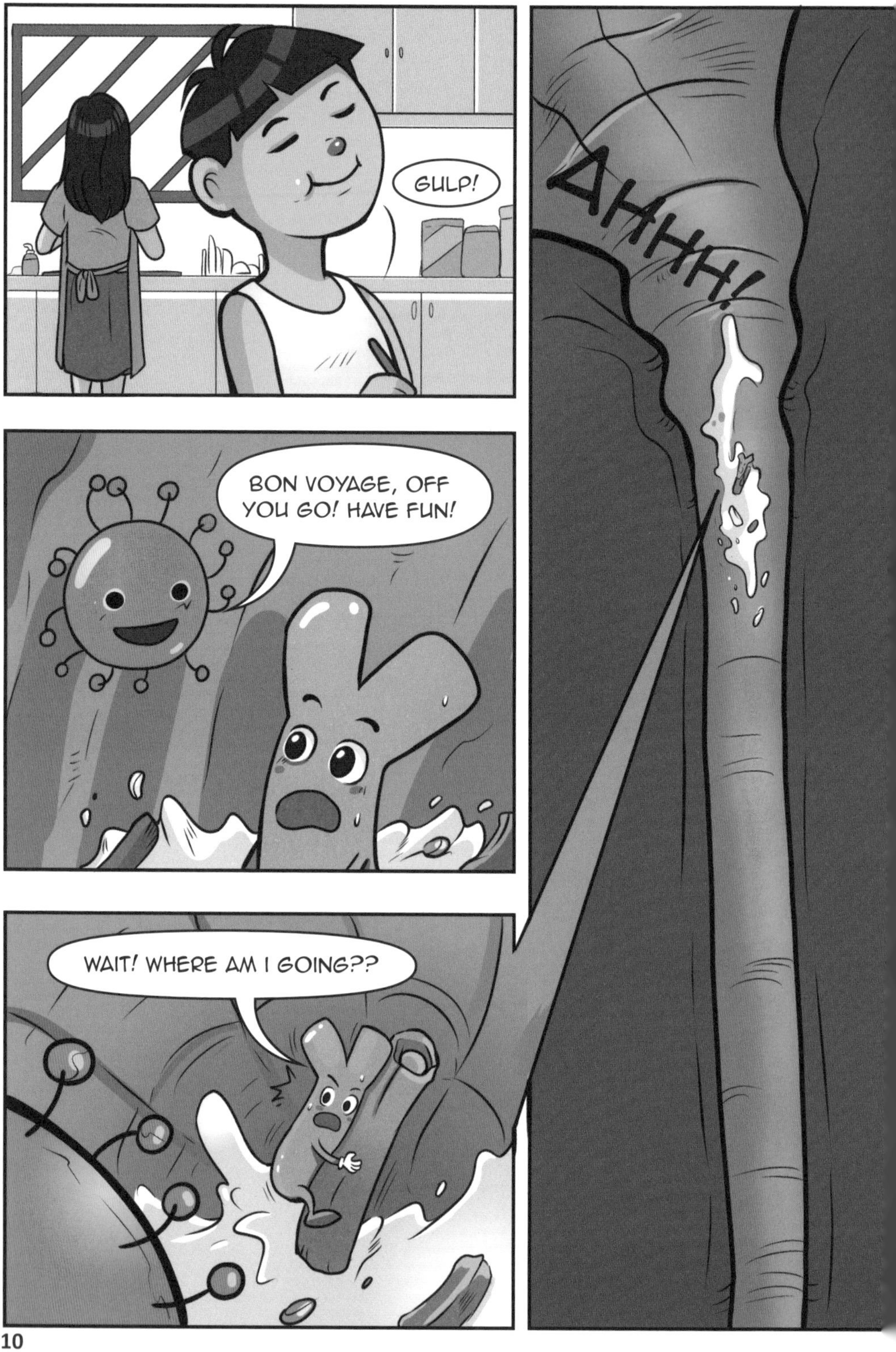
GULP!
BON VOYAGE, OFF YOU GO! HAVE FUN!
WAIT! WHERE AM I GOING??
AHHH!

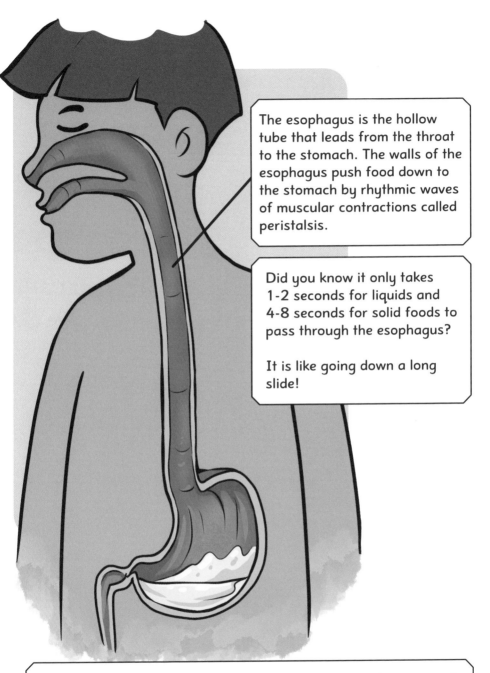

The esophagus is the hollow tube that leads from the throat to the stomach. The walls of the esophagus push food down to the stomach by rhythmic waves of muscular contractions called peristalsis.

Did you know it only takes 1-2 seconds for liquids and 4-8 seconds for solid foods to pass through the esophagus?

It is like going down a long slide!

Not all bacteria are bad! There are plenty of bacteria living in and on our body, and most of them are in fact good for our health! For example, bacteria play essential roles in helping us digest the food we eat, which we will learn more about as Guss' story unfolds...

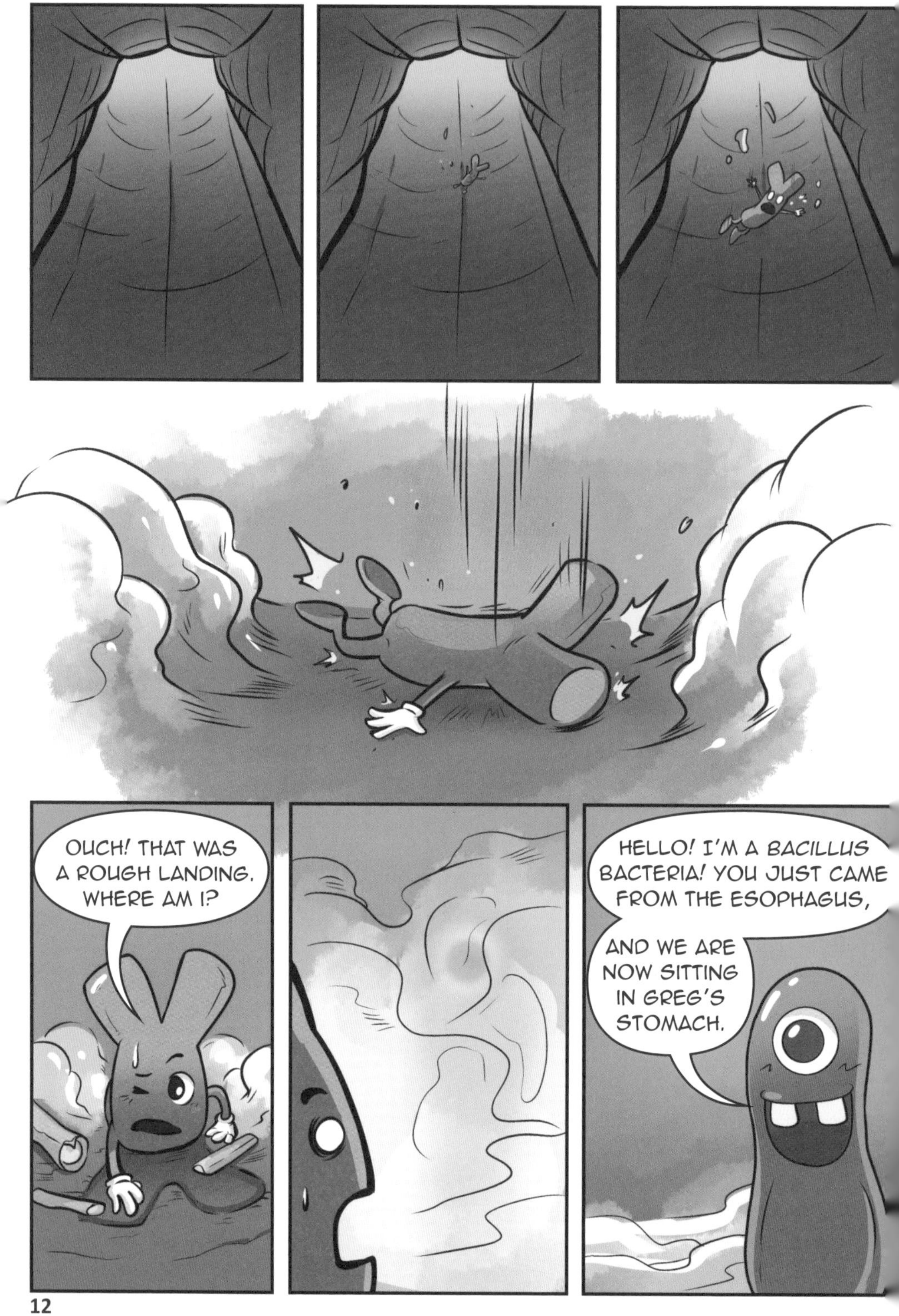
OUCH! THAT WAS A ROUGH LANDING. WHERE AM I?
HELLO! I'M A BACILLUS BACTERIA! YOU JUST CAME FROM THE ESOPHAGUS,
AND WE ARE NOW SITTING IN GREG'S STOMACH.

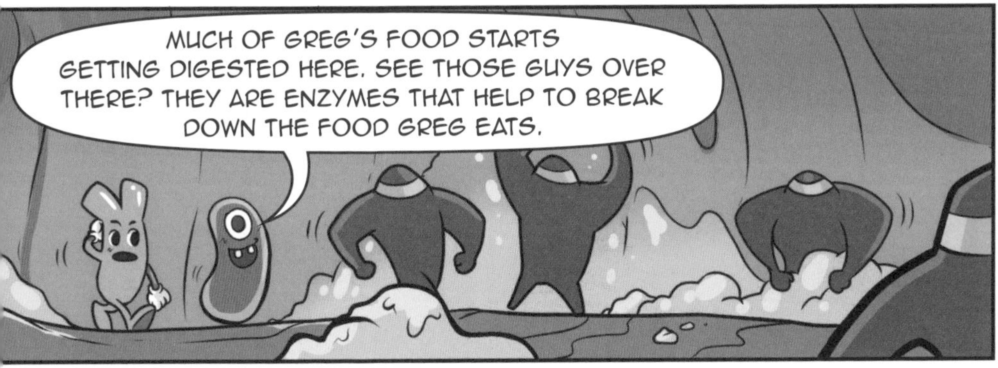
MUCH OF GREG'S FOOD STARTS GETTING DIGESTED HERE. SEE THOSE GUYS OVER THERE? THEY ARE ENZYMES THAT HELP TO BREAK DOWN THE FOOD GREG EATS.

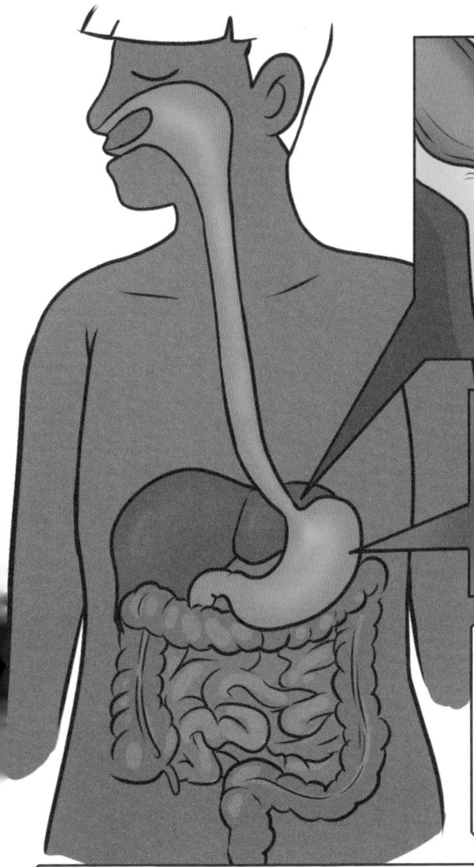

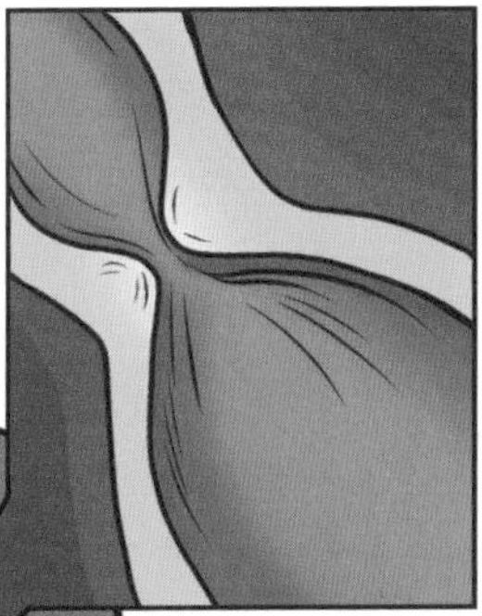

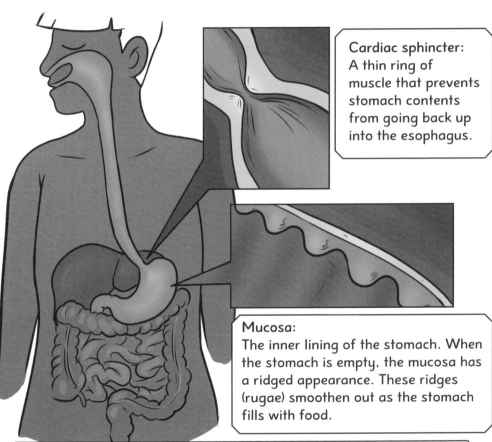

Cardiac sphincter:
A thin ring of muscle that prevents stomach contents from going back up into the esophagus.

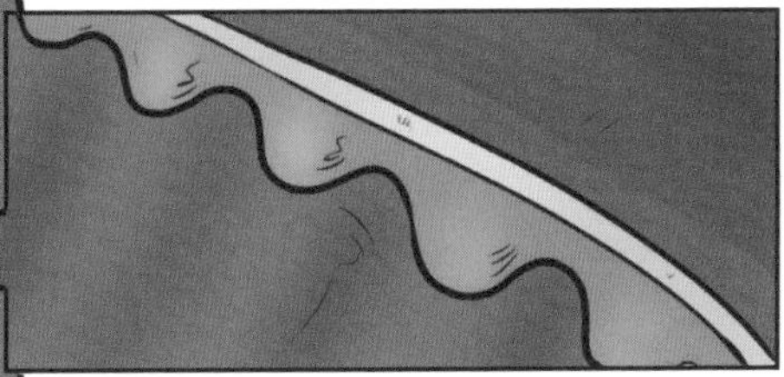

Mucosa:
The inner lining of the stomach. When the stomach is empty, the mucosa has a ridged appearance. These ridges (rugae) smoothen out as the stomach fills with food.

The mucosa contains special cells that produce acids and enzymes like pepsin to help digest food. The mucosa also releases mucus to protect the lining of the stomach from the digestive acids. Other special cells in the mucosa release hormones into the blood that control gastric acid production, appetite and stomach churning.

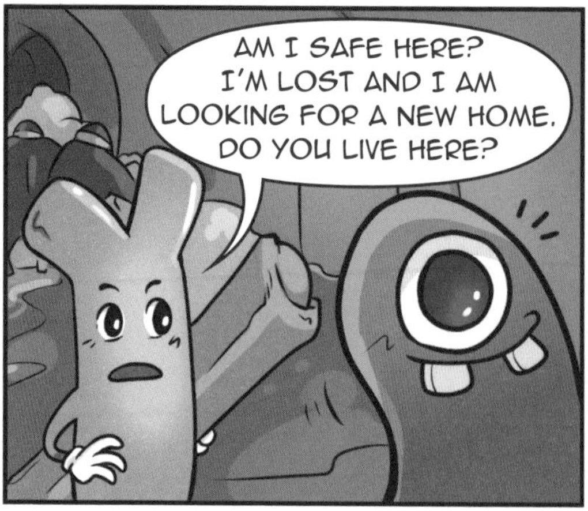
AM I SAFE HERE? I'M LOST AND I AM LOOKING FOR A NEW HOME. DO YOU LIVE HERE?

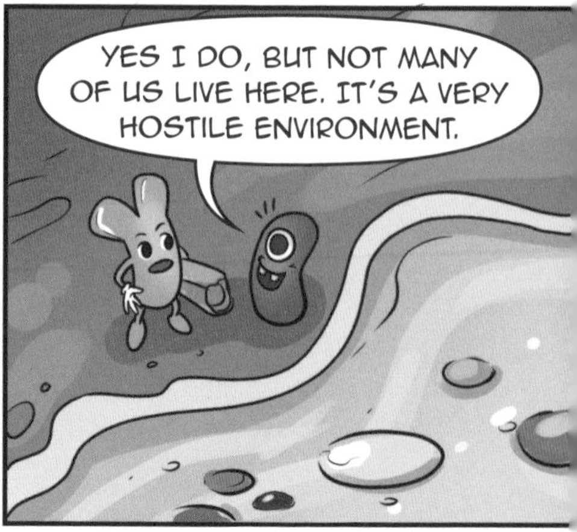
YES I DO, BUT NOT MANY OF US LIVE HERE. IT'S A VERY HOSTILE ENVIRONMENT.

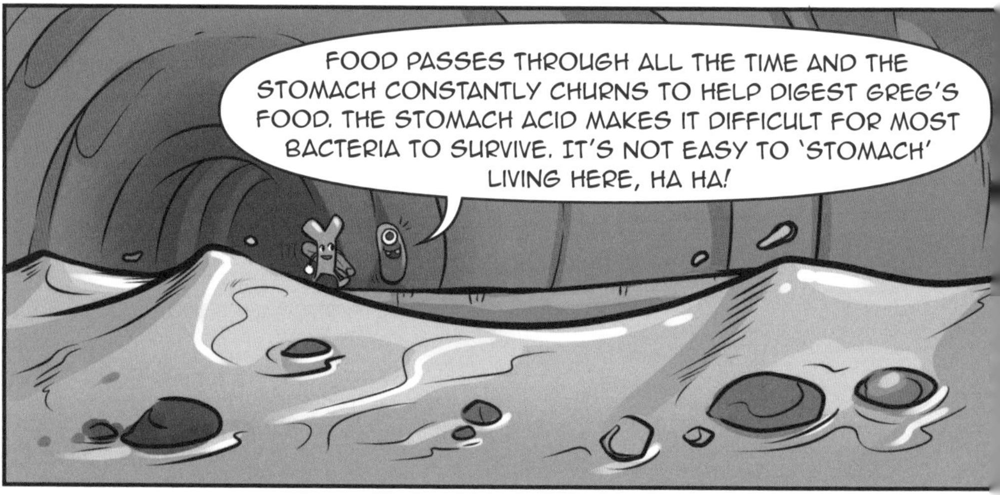
FOOD PASSES THROUGH ALL THE TIME AND THE STOMACH CONSTANTLY CHURNS TO HELP DIGEST GREG'S FOOD. THE STOMACH ACID MAKES IT DIFFICULT FOR MOST BACTERIA TO SURVIVE. IT'S NOT EASY TO 'STOMACH' LIVING HERE, HA HA!

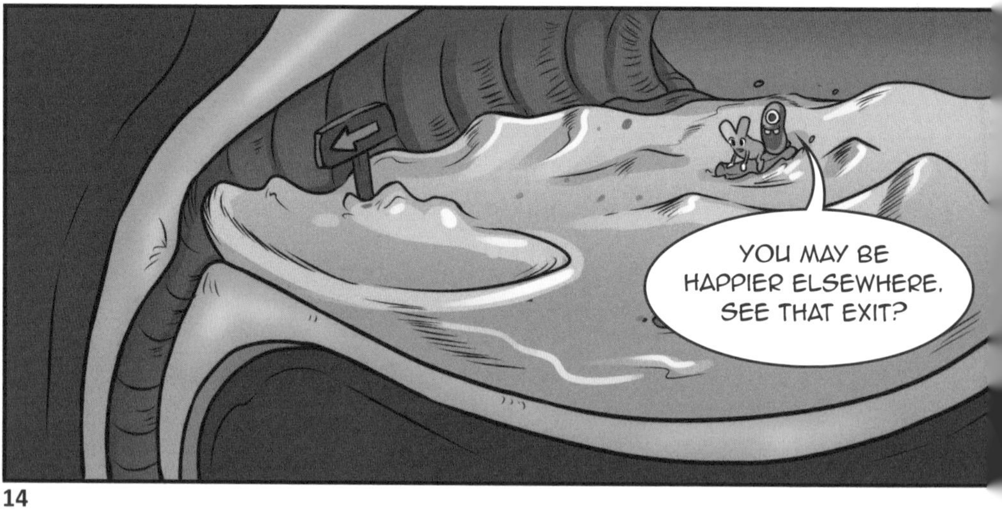
YOU MAY BE HAPPIER ELSEWHERE. SEE THAT EXIT?

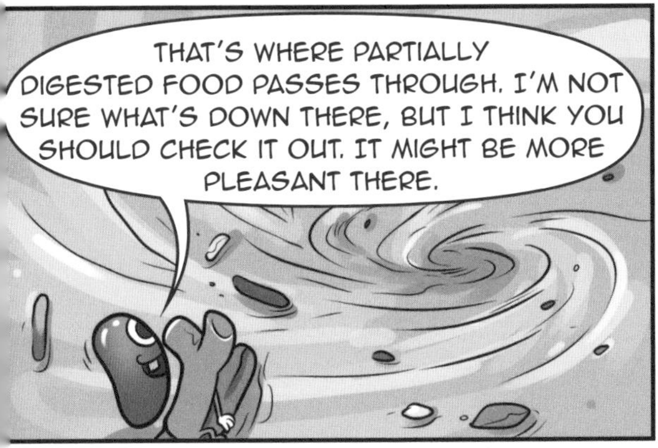
THAT'S WHERE PARTIALLY DIGESTED FOOD PASSES THROUGH. I'M NOT SURE WHAT'S DOWN THERE, BUT I THINK YOU SHOULD CHECK IT OUT. IT MIGHT BE MORE PLEASANT THERE.

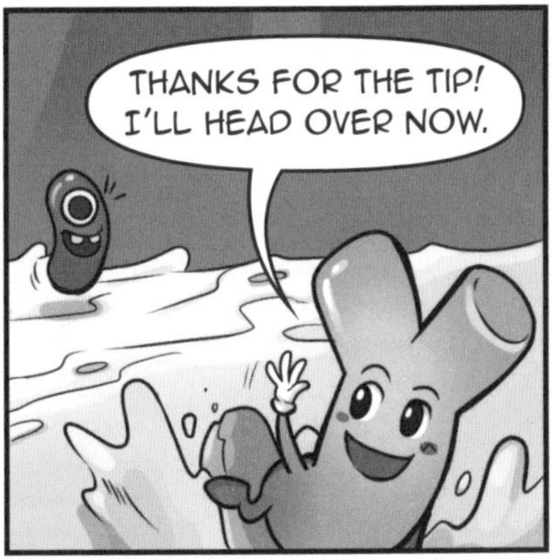
THANKS FOR THE TIP! I'LL HEAD OVER NOW.

Chyme: Food that has been mixed and broken down by enzymes into a thick, soupy mixture.

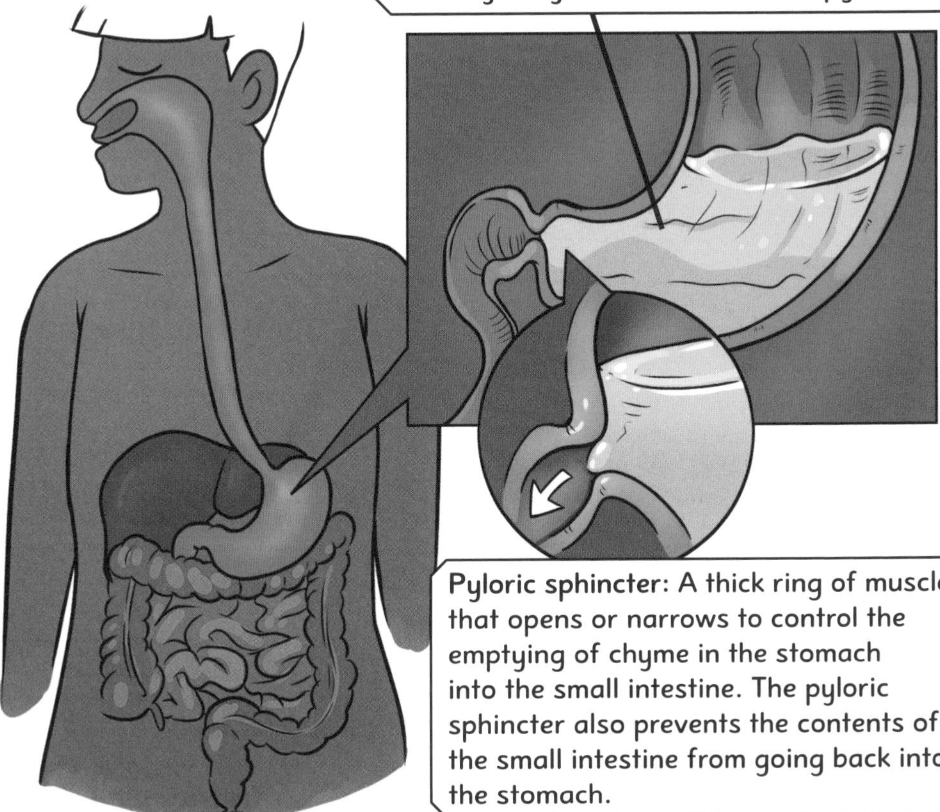

Pyloric sphincter: A thick ring of muscle that opens or narrows to control the emptying of chyme in the stomach into the small intestine. The pyloric sphincter also prevents the contents of the small intestine from going back into the stomach.

The stomach helps to store food temporarily for 2-4 hours. While food is in the stomach, it is broken down into chyme by the contraction and relaxation of muscles in the stomach. The stomach does not play a big role in absorbing food. It only absorbs water, alcohol and some drugs.

WOW, IT SURE IS NARROW AND WINDING IN HERE...

HELLO FRIENDS! I'M NEW AROUND HERE. WHERE AM I?

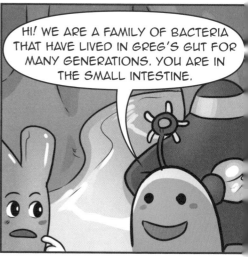

HI! WE ARE A FAMILY OF BACTERIA THAT HAVE LIVED IN GREG'S GUT FOR MANY GENERATIONS. YOU ARE IN THE SMALL INTESTINE.

HERE, WE CONTINUE DIGESTING GREG'S FOOD WITH THE HELP OF MORE ENZYMES.

MOST OF DIGESTION HAPPENS HERE.

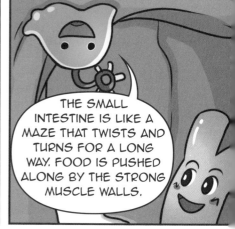

THE SMALL INTESTINE IS LIKE A MAZE THAT TWISTS AND TURNS FOR A LONG WAY. FOOD IS PUSHED ALONG BY THE STRONG MUSCLE WALLS.

The small intestine stretches out to seven metres long! It is the main site of digestion and absorption, making it the workhorse of the gastrointestinal tract.

The small intestine is divided into three parts — the duodenum, the jejunum and the ileum.

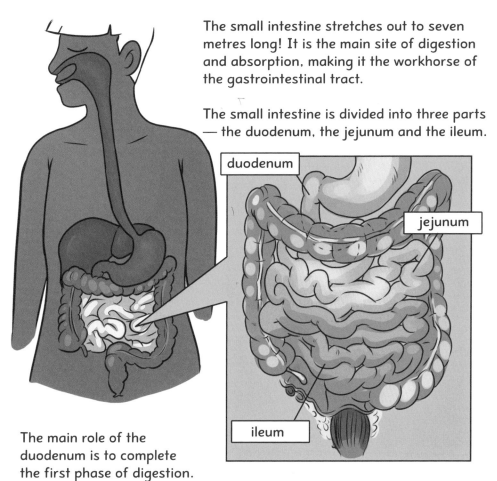

duodenum

jejunum

ileum

The main role of the duodenum is to complete the first phase of digestion.
In this section of the intestine, food from the stomach is mixed with enzymes from the pancreas and bile from the gall bladder. The enzymes and bile help break down food.

Main food groups and enzymes catalysing digestion in the small intestine: carbohydrates (amylase, maltase), protein (peptidase, trypsin), fat (lipase).

Enzymes in the small intestine work best at basic pH (> 7). The pancreas produces a substance to help neutralise chyme from the acidic stomach. Bile helps with this as well.

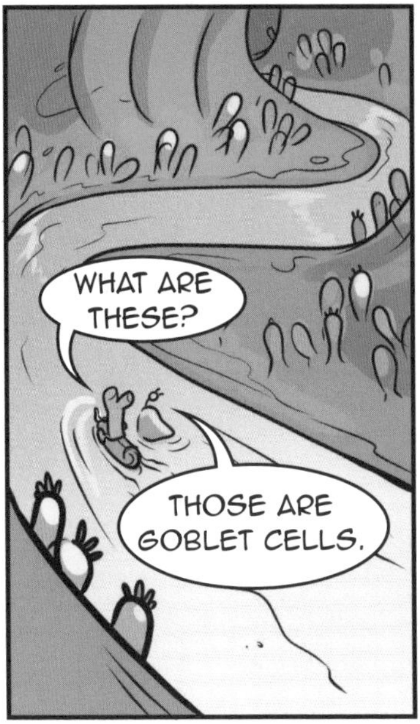
WHAT ARE THESE?
THOSE ARE GOBLET CELLS.

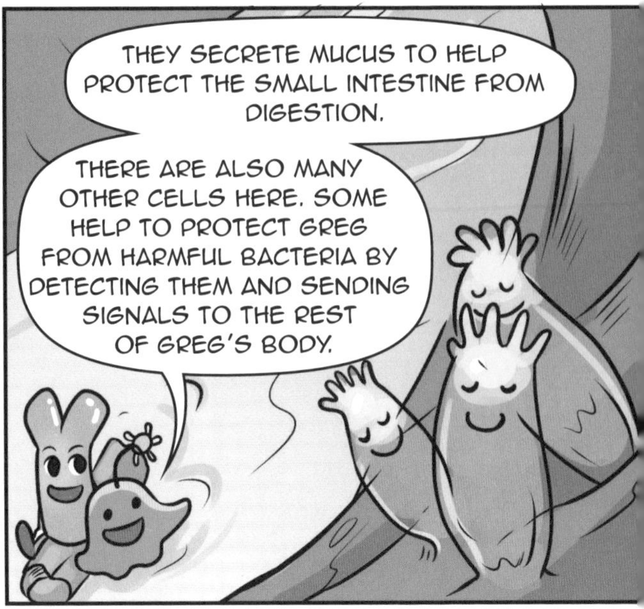
THEY SECRETE MUCUS TO HELP PROTECT THE SMALL INTESTINE FROM DIGESTION.
THERE ARE ALSO MANY OTHER CELLS HERE. SOME HELP TO PROTECT GREG FROM HARMFUL BACTERIA BY DETECTING THEM AND SENDING SIGNALS TO THE REST OF GREG'S BODY.

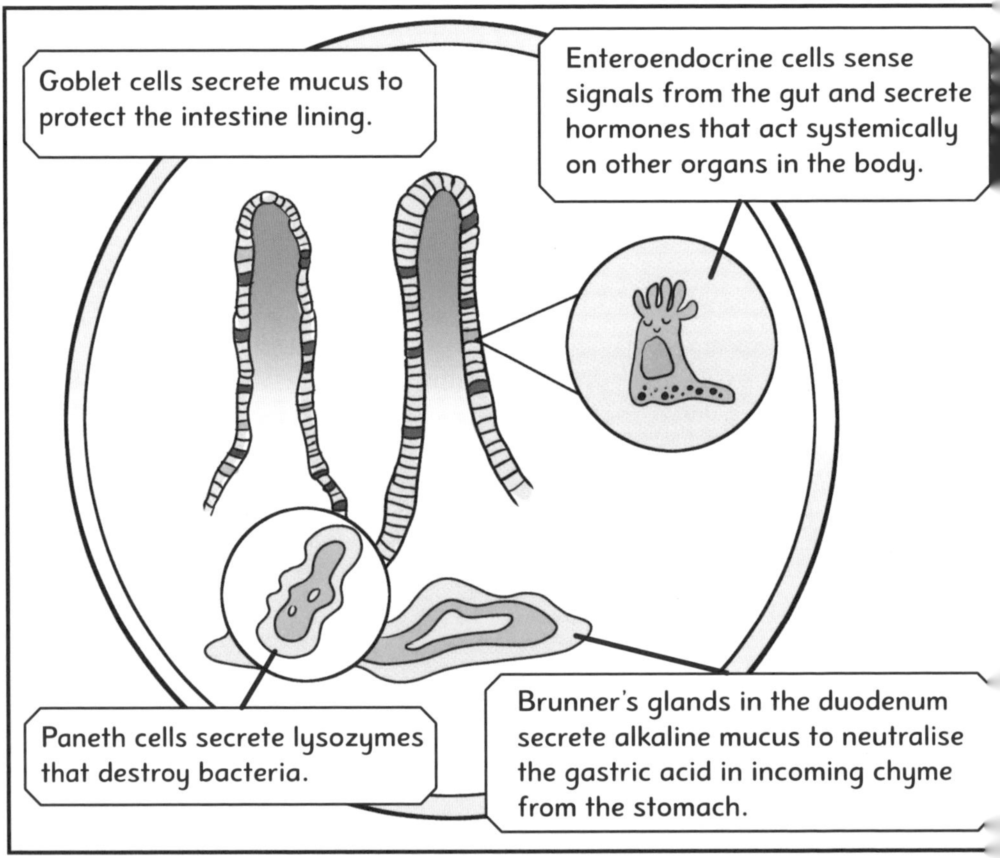
Goblet cells secrete mucus to protect the intestine lining.
Enteroendocrine cells sense signals from the gut and secrete hormones that act systemically on other organs in the body.
Paneth cells secrete lysozymes that destroy bacteria.
Brunner's glands in the duodenum secrete alkaline mucus to neutralise the gastric acid in incoming chyme from the stomach.

IT SURE SOUNDS BUSY IN HERE!

INDEED.

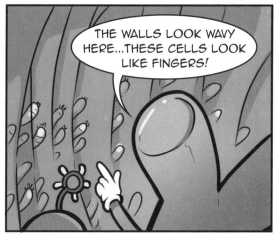

THE WALLS LOOK WAVY HERE...THESE CELLS LOOK LIKE FINGERS!

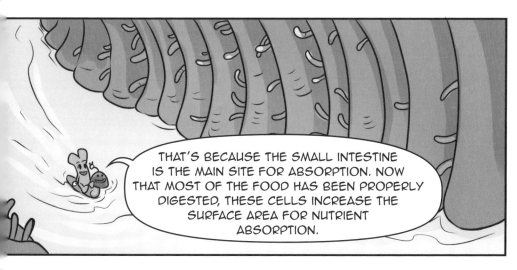

THAT'S BECAUSE THE SMALL INTESTINE IS THE MAIN SITE FOR ABSORPTION. NOW THAT MOST OF THE FOOD HAS BEEN PROPERLY DIGESTED, THESE CELLS INCREASE THE SURFACE AREA FOR NUTRIENT ABSORPTION.

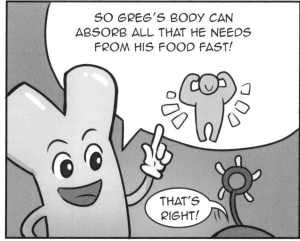

SO GREG'S BODY CAN ABSORB ALL THAT HE NEEDS FROM HIS FOOD FAST!

THAT'S RIGHT!

After food is broken down in the duodenum, it moves into the jejunum.

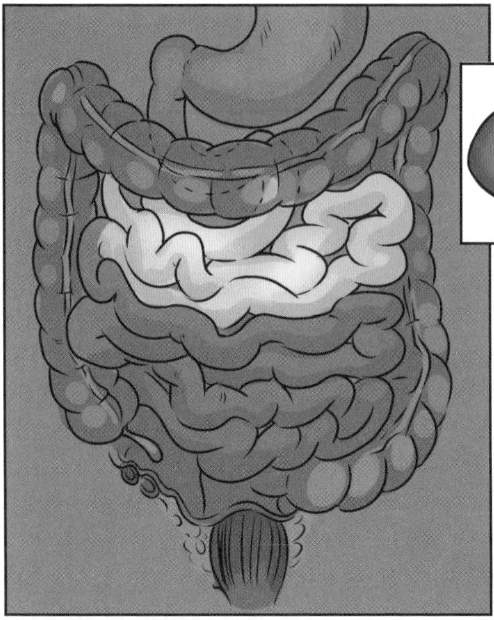

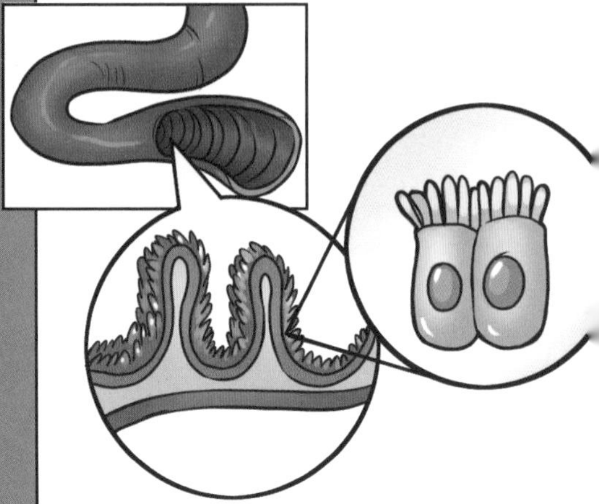

The inside walls of the jejunum have many folds called villi, which make its surface area large enough to absorb the various nutrients that the body needs. The cells along these folds contain additional projections called microvilli to further increase the surface area for absorption.

With these handy organisational tricks, the absorptive surface area of the small intestine is actually around 250 square metres, the size of a tennis court!

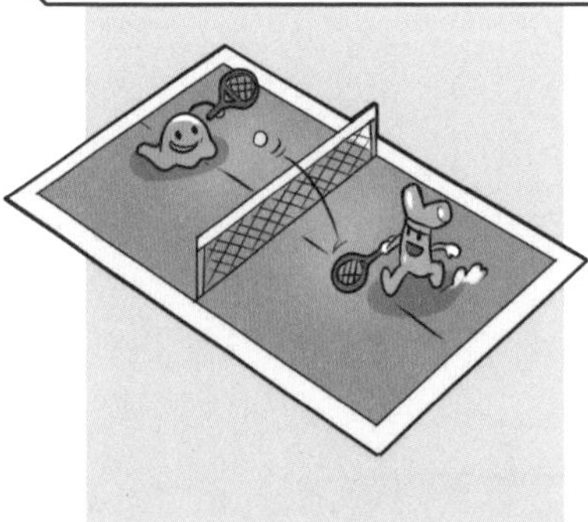

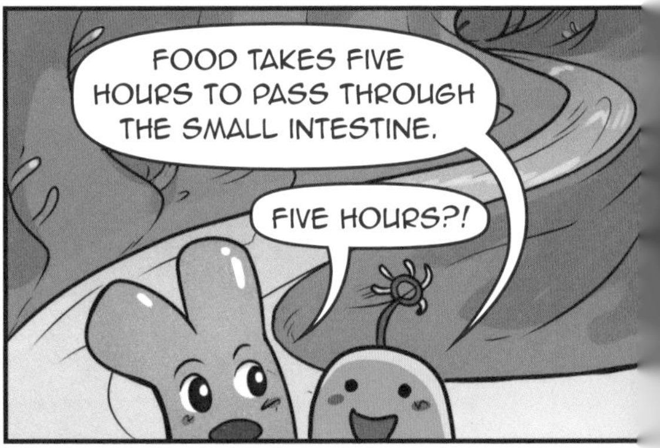
FOOD TAKES FIVE HOURS TO PASS THROUGH THE SMALL INTESTINE.
FIVE HOURS?!

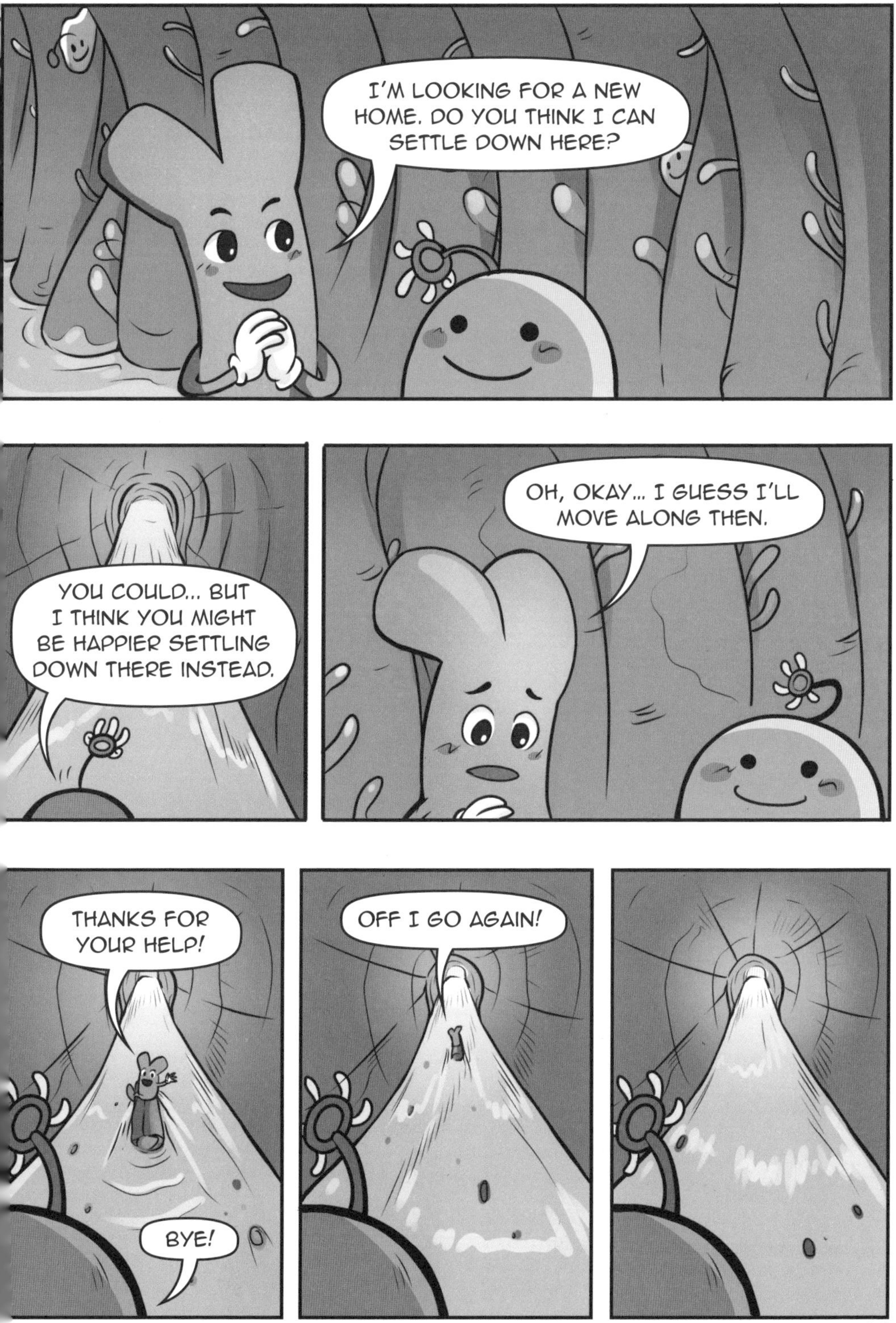
I'M LOOKING FOR A NEW HOME. DO YOU THINK I CAN SETTLE DOWN HERE?
YOU COULD... BUT I THINK YOU MIGHT BE HAPPIER SETTLING DOWN THERE INSTEAD.
OH, OKAY... I GUESS I'LL MOVE ALONG THEN.
THANKS FOR YOUR HELP!
BYE!
OFF I GO AGAIN!

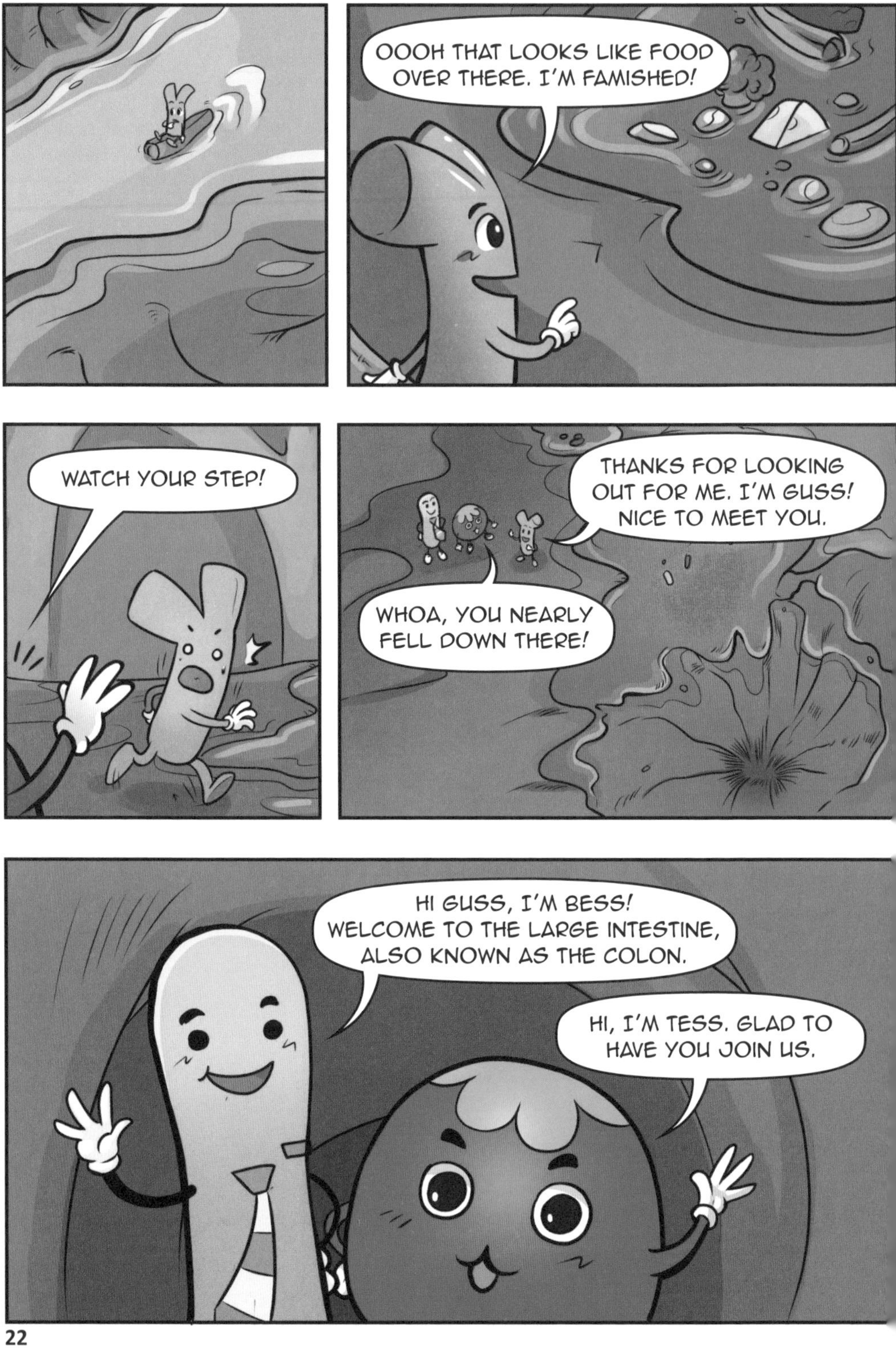
OOOH THAT LOOKS LIKE FOOD OVER THERE. I'M FAMISHED!
WATCH YOUR STEP!
WHOA, YOU NEARLY FELL DOWN THERE!
THANKS FOR LOOKING OUT FOR ME. I'M GUSS! NICE TO MEET YOU.
HI GUSS, I'M BESS! WELCOME TO THE LARGE INTESTINE, ALSO KNOWN AS THE COLON.
HI, I'M TESS. GLAD TO HAVE YOU JOIN US.

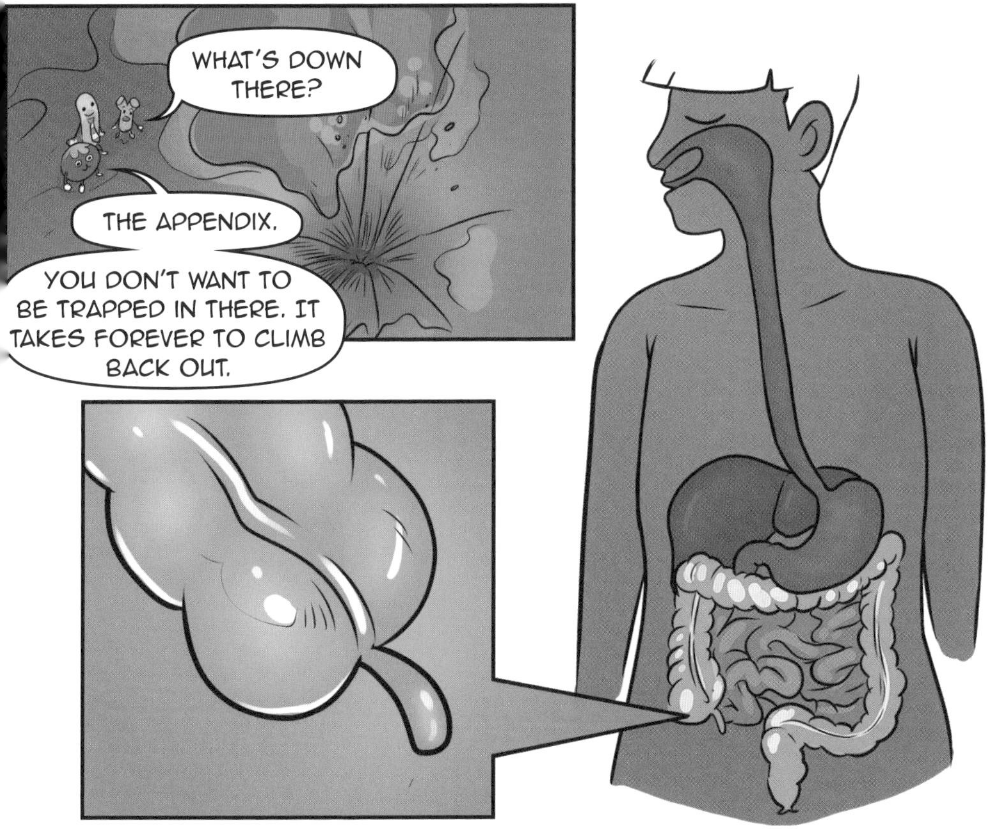
WHAT'S DOWN THERE?
THE APPENDIX.
YOU DON'T WANT TO BE TRAPPED IN THERE. IT TAKES FOREVER TO CLIMB BACK OUT.

The appendix is a mystery organ! Some scientists believe this little pocket is a mere remnant from our evolutionary past with no function, but other experts have suggested that the appendix acts as a safe house for good bacteria.

A bout of severe diarrhoea can affect your gut microbiome. The appendix repopulates and reboots the intestine with good bacteria before harmful bacteria find a home there. Humans aren't the only animals with an appendix; more than 500 other mammals live with an appendix too!

Bacteria in the digestive system come in various shapes and sizes! Here are some common forms:

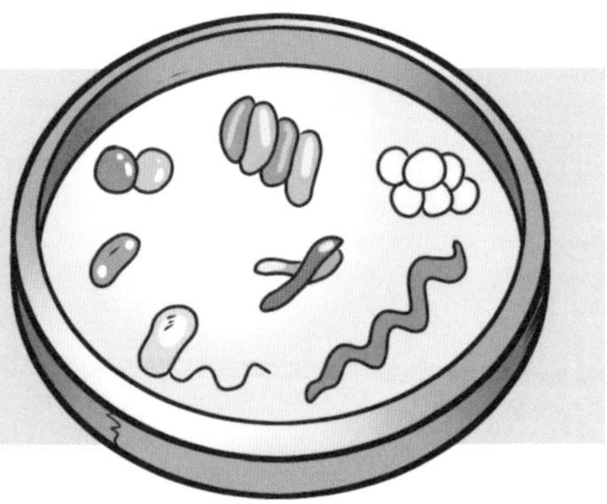

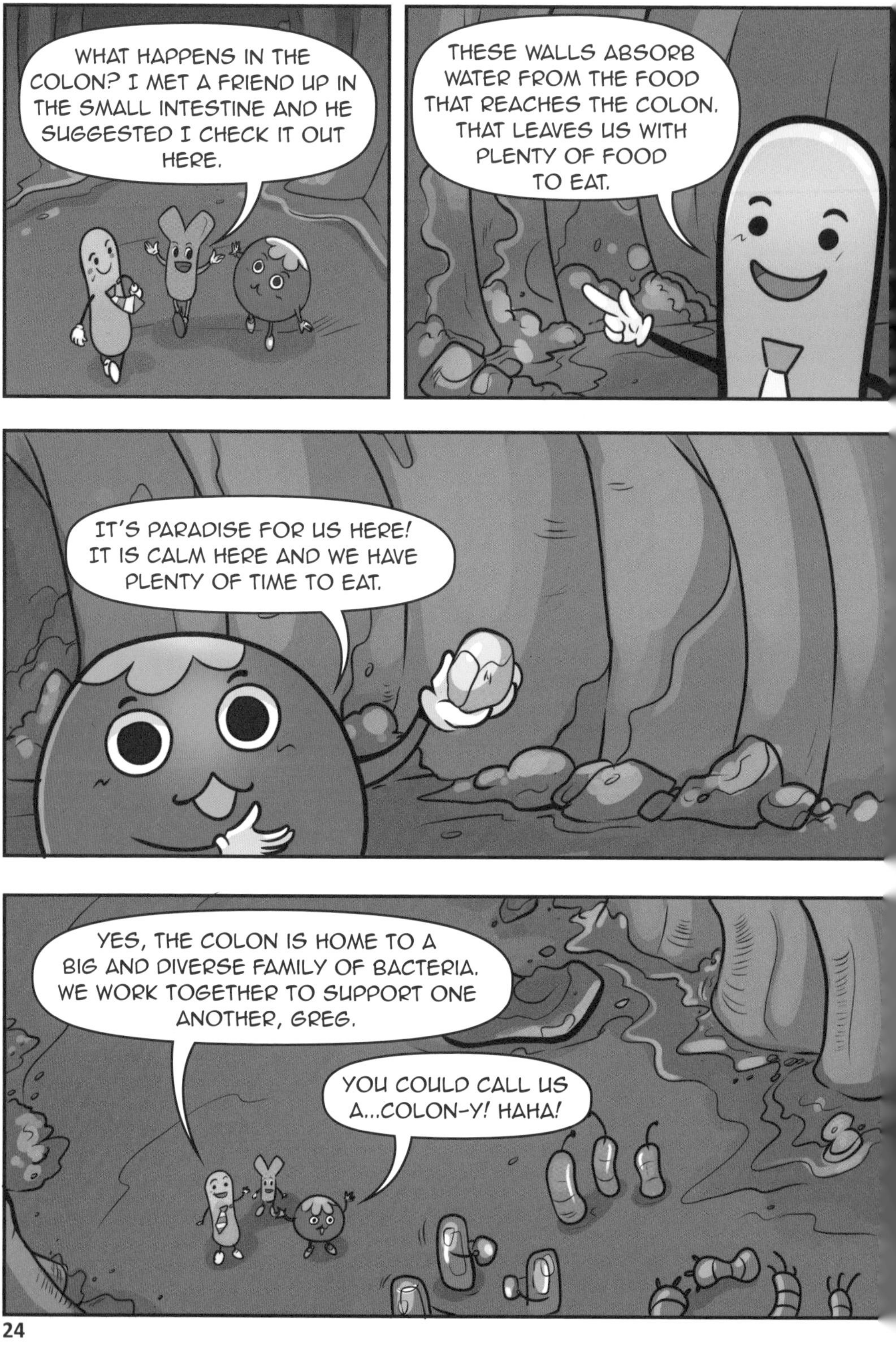
WHAT HAPPENS IN THE COLON? I MET A FRIEND UP IN THE SMALL INTESTINE AND HE SUGGESTED I CHECK IT OUT HERE.
THESE WALLS ABSORB WATER FROM THE FOOD THAT REACHES THE COLON. THAT LEAVES US WITH PLENTY OF FOOD TO EAT.
IT'S PARADISE FOR US HERE! IT IS CALM HERE AND WE HAVE PLENTY OF TIME TO EAT.
YES, THE COLON IS HOME TO A BIG AND DIVERSE FAMILY OF BACTERIA. WE WORK TOGETHER TO SUPPORT ONE ANOTHER, GREG.
YOU COULD CALL US A...COLON-Y! HAHA!

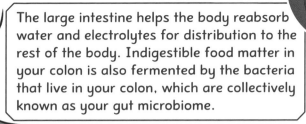

The large intestine helps the body reabsorb water and electrolytes for distribution to the rest of the body. Indigestible food matter in your colon is also fermented by the bacteria that live in your colon, which are collectively known as your gut microbiome.

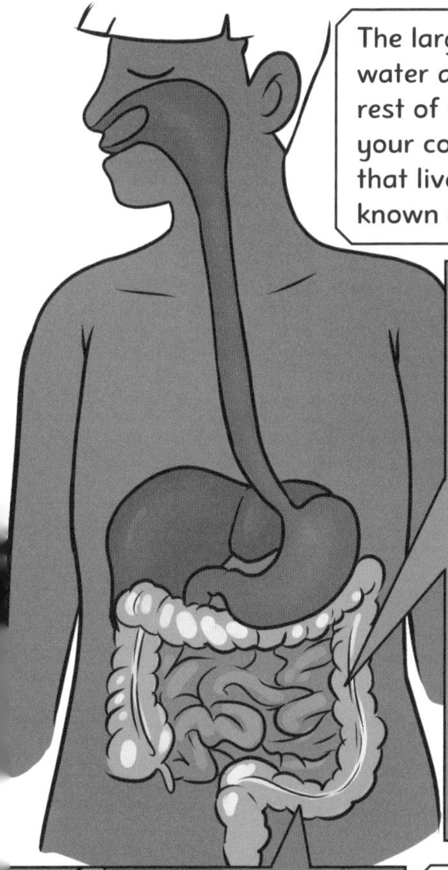

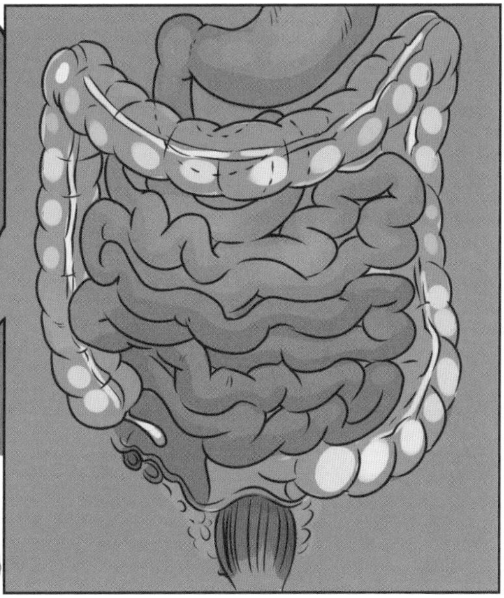

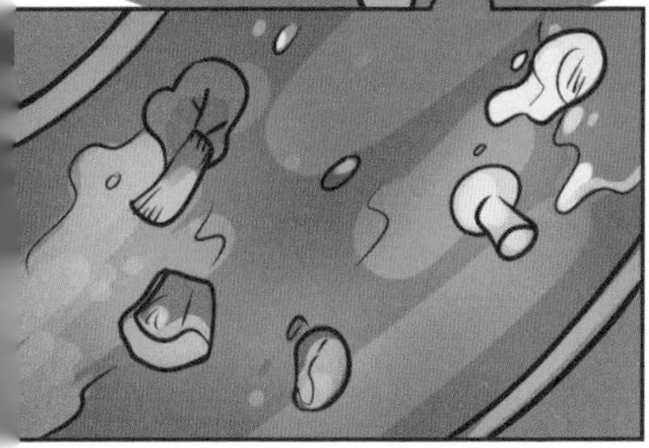

Leftover undigested food is packed tightly and stored in the sigmoid colon as faeces until it finally exits the rectum. Food spends between 20-50 hours in the large intestine, depending on what you eat!

There are more than 10 bacteria for every human cell in your body. Your gut bacteria weigh up to 2 kg!

Apart from bacteria like Guss, Bess and Tess, our gut is home to several other types of bacteria, even bad ones. Some examples of bad bacteria are *Camphylobacter* (spiral shaped) and *Clostridium* (rod shaped), whom we will meet later!

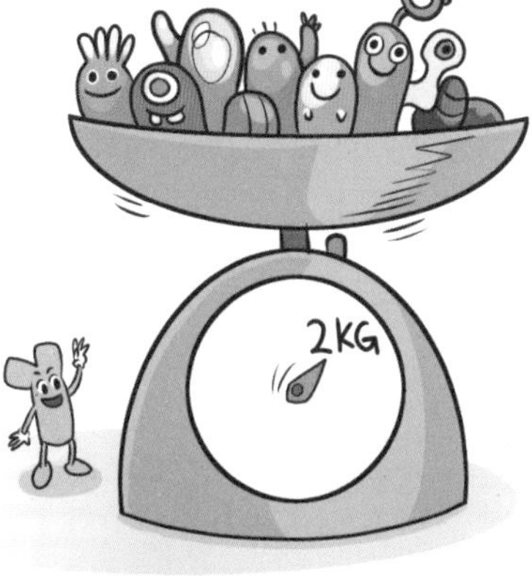
2KG

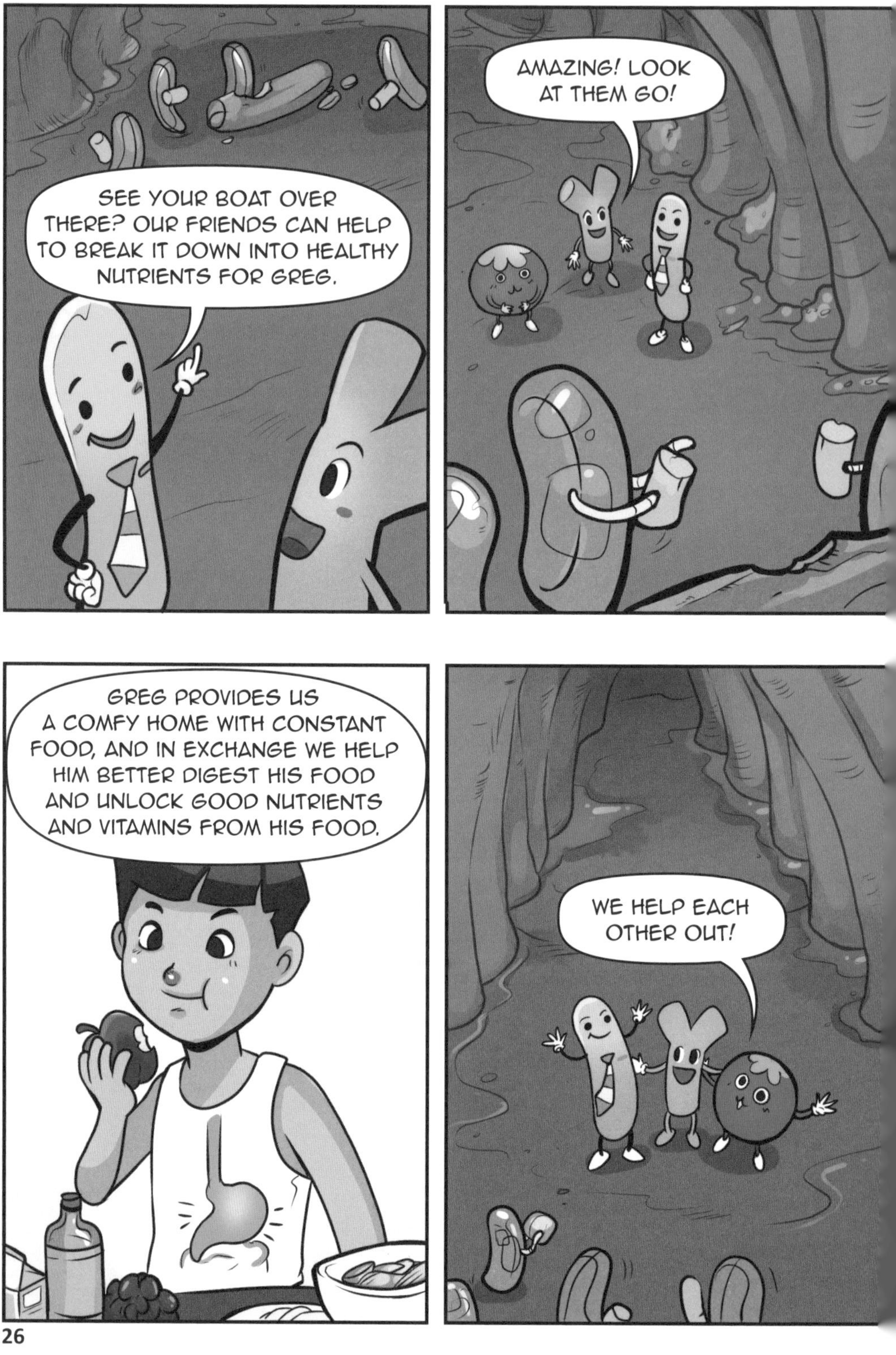
SEE YOUR BOAT OVER THERE? OUR FRIENDS CAN HELP TO BREAK IT DOWN INTO HEALTHY NUTRIENTS FOR GREG.
AMAZING! LOOK AT THEM GO!
GREG PROVIDES US A COMFY HOME WITH CONSTANT FOOD, AND IN EXCHANGE WE HELP HIM BETTER DIGEST HIS FOOD AND UNLOCK GOOD NUTRIENTS AND VITAMINS FROM HIS FOOD.
WE HELP EACH OTHER OUT!

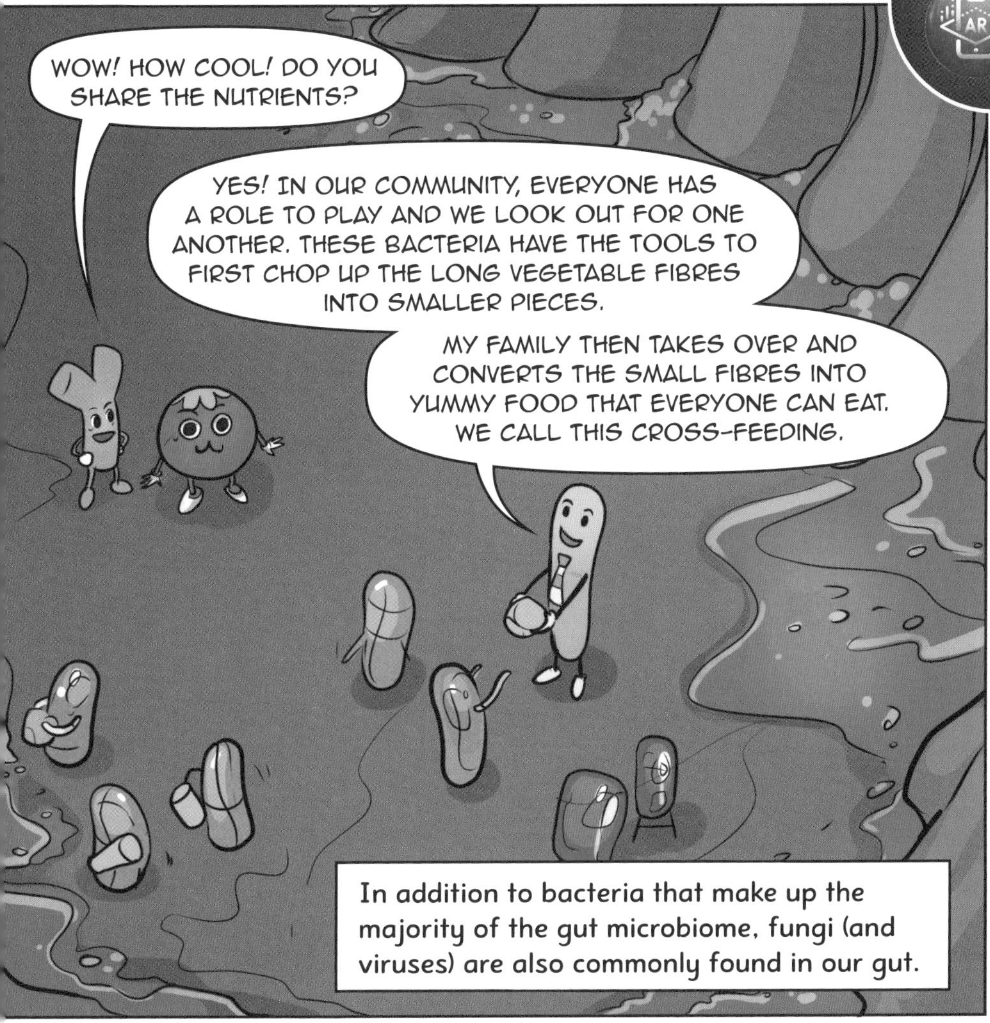
WOW! HOW COOL! DO YOU SHARE THE NUTRIENTS?
YES! IN OUR COMMUNITY, EVERYONE HAS A ROLE TO PLAY AND WE LOOK OUT FOR ONE ANOTHER. THESE BACTERIA HAVE THE TOOLS TO FIRST CHOP UP THE LONG VEGETABLE FIBRES INTO SMALLER PIECES.
MY FAMILY THEN TAKES OVER AND CONVERTS THE SMALL FIBRES INTO YUMMY FOOD THAT EVERYONE CAN EAT. WE CALL THIS CROSS-FEEDING.
In addition to bacteria that make up the majority of the gut microbiome, fungi (and viruses) are also commonly found in our gut.

The bacteria in your gut microbiome help digest your food, regulate your immune system, protect against other bacteria that cause disease and produce essential vitamins.

Good gut bacteria produce messenger molecules that help educate our immune system to co-exist harmoniously and stimulate gut cell regeneration. Some molecules produced by gut bacteria, e.g., serotonin, even communicate with our brain as well!

Despite playing such critical roles in health, the gut microbiome was not generally recognised to exist until the late 1990s!

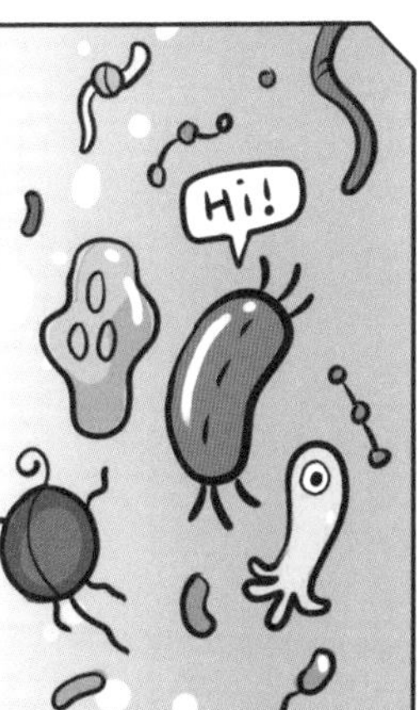
Hi!

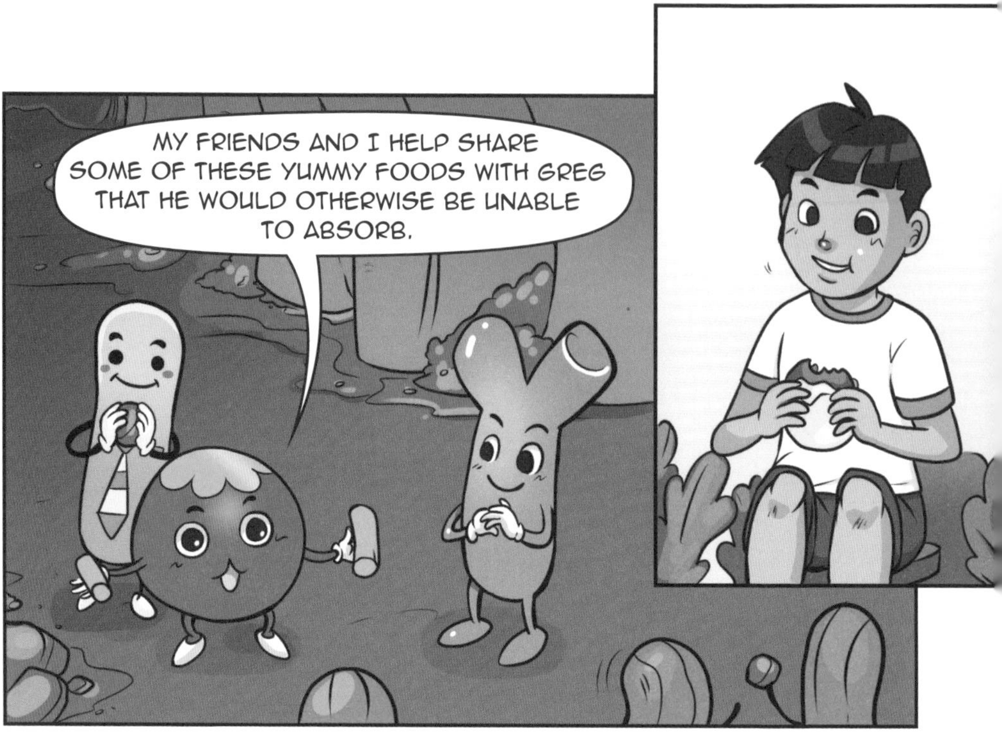
MY FRIENDS AND I HELP SHARE SOME OF THESE YUMMY FOODS WITH GREG THAT HE WOULD OTHERWISE BE UNABLE TO ABSORB.
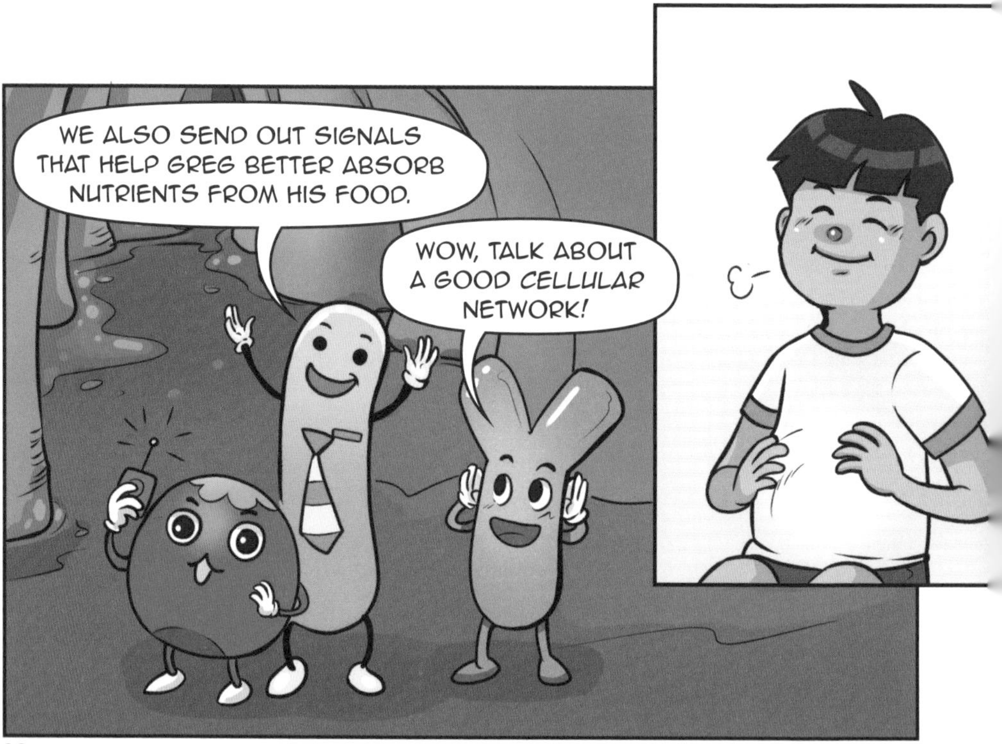
WE ALSO SEND OUT SIGNALS THAT HELP GREG BETTER ABSORB NUTRIENTS FROM HIS FOOD.
WOW, TALK ABOUT A GOOD CELLULAR NETWORK!

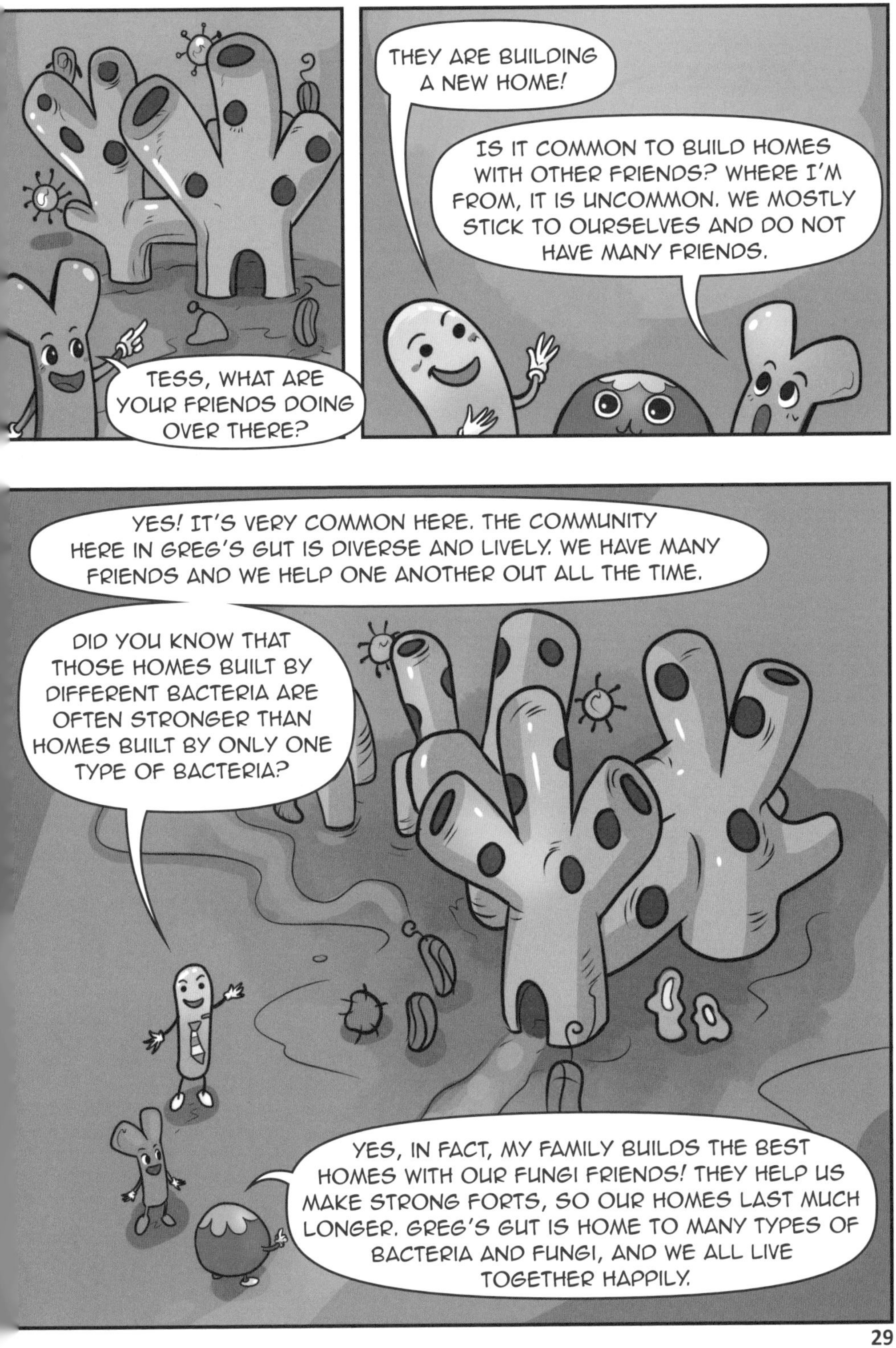
TESS, WHAT ARE YOUR FRIENDS DOING OVER THERE?
THEY ARE BUILDING A NEW HOME!
IS IT COMMON TO BUILD HOMES WITH OTHER FRIENDS? WHERE I'M FROM, IT IS UNCOMMON. WE MOSTLY STICK TO OURSELVES AND DO NOT HAVE MANY FRIENDS.
YES! IT'S VERY COMMON HERE. THE COMMUNITY HERE IN GREG'S GUT IS DIVERSE AND LIVELY. WE HAVE MANY FRIENDS AND WE HELP ONE ANOTHER OUT ALL THE TIME.
DID YOU KNOW THAT THOSE HOMES BUILT BY DIFFERENT BACTERIA ARE OFTEN STRONGER THAN HOMES BUILT BY ONLY ONE TYPE OF BACTERIA?
YES, IN FACT, MY FAMILY BUILDS THE BEST HOMES WITH OUR FUNGI FRIENDS! THEY HELP US MAKE STRONG FORTS, SO OUR HOMES LAST MUCH LONGER. GREG'S GUT IS HOME TO MANY TYPES OF BACTERIA AND FUNGI, AND WE ALL LIVE TOGETHER HAPPILY.

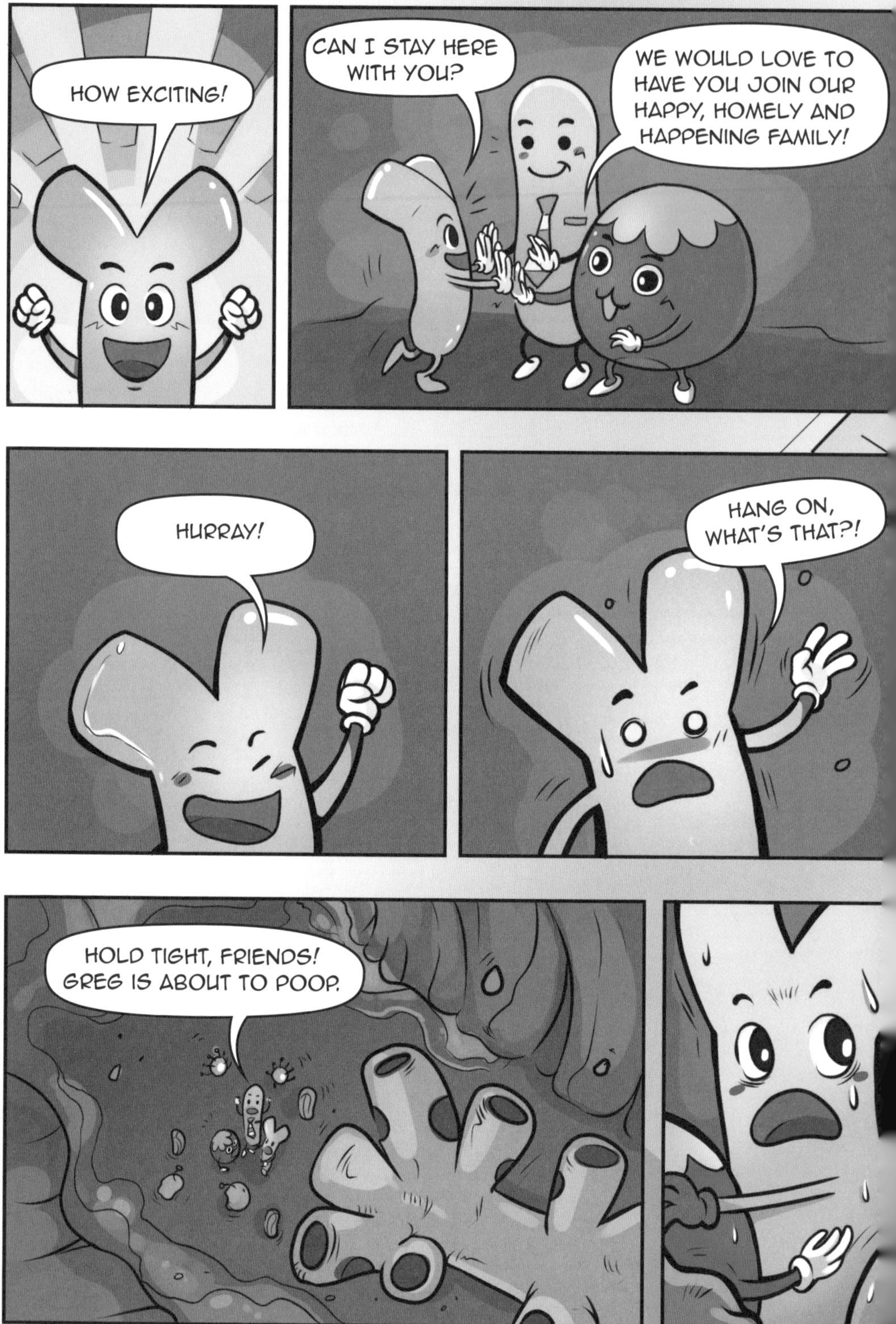
HOW EXCITING!
CAN I STAY HERE WITH YOU?
WE WOULD LOVE TO HAVE YOU JOIN OUR HAPPY, HOMELY AND HAPPENING FAMILY!
HURRAY!
HANG ON, WHAT'S THAT?!
HOLD TIGHT, FRIENDS! GREG IS ABOUT TO POOP.

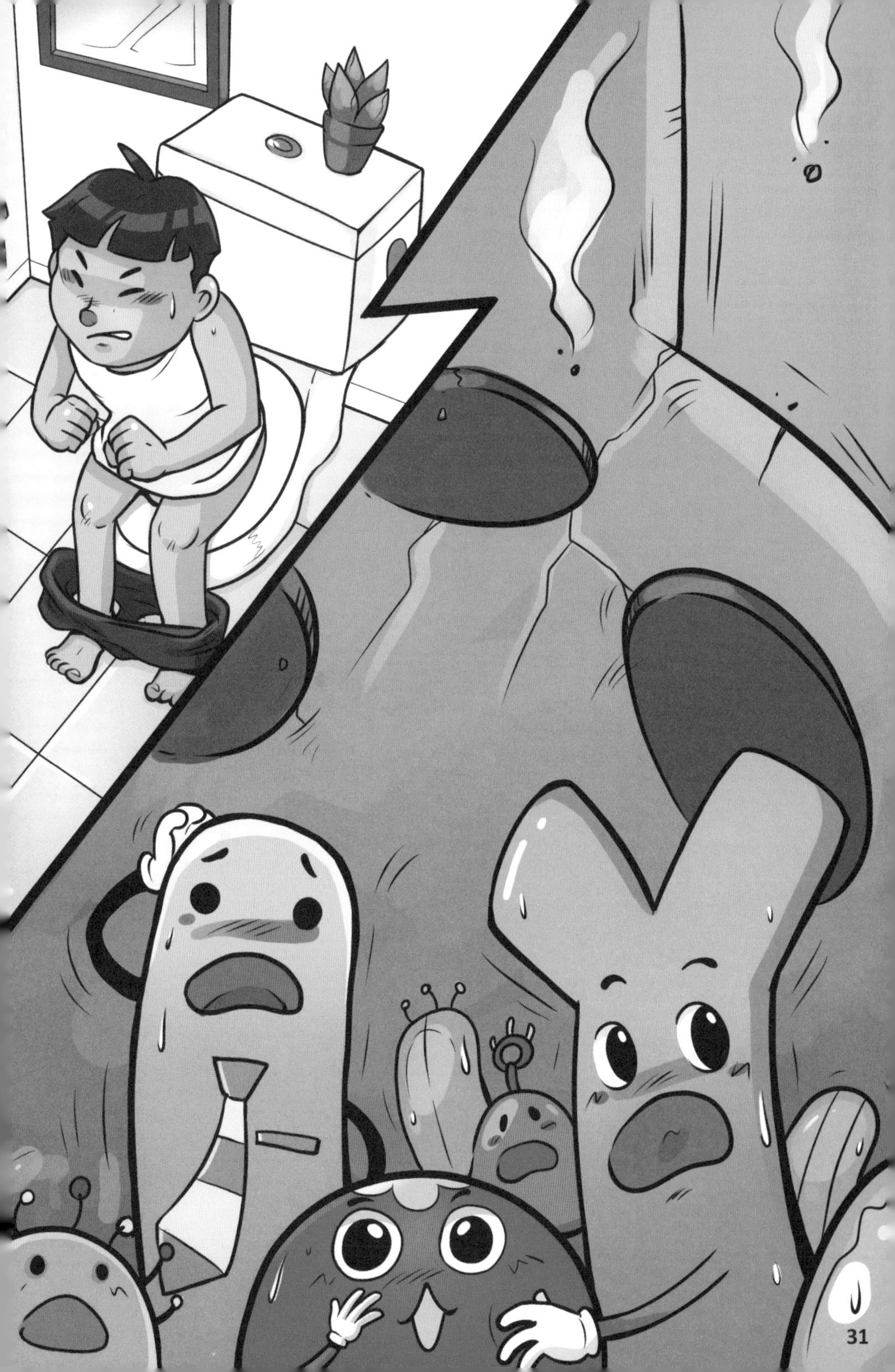

Fun Fact 1

Did you know that apart from our guts, microbes also live on many other surfaces in and on our body? Bacteria and fungi are found on our skin, head, lungs and eyes and often co-exist happily without causing us harm. Some sites, such as our lungs and eyes, have much less diverse microbial communities. At such places, there are various active measures to keep microbial communities in check.

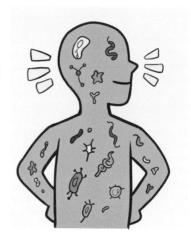

Fun Fact 2

Have you ever wondered why we fart? This is caused by a process known as fermentation, where bacteria break down the food we eat so that we can better absorb the nutrients in our food. During this process, bacteria produce various gases in our gut, which are eventually expelled, in the form of a fart! Methane, which is one of the gases, contributes to the distinctive smell of a fart.

Fun Fact 3

Bacteria such as *Lactobacillus* and *Bifidobacterium* are essential to the production of yogurt. They help to break down the simple sugar lactose in milk into lactic acid, which contributes to the sour and tart taste of yogurt. By breaking down lactose found in milk, many people who are lactose-intolerant and unable to drink milk can still consume yogurt and reap its health benefits!

Make Your Own Yogurt!

Did you know you can make or "grow" your own yogurt at home? Try it out!

1. Heat milk up to 80°C (scalding the milk first removes any bad bacteria and promotes a richer end product), and let it cool back down to 40°C (to avoid killing the good bacteria).

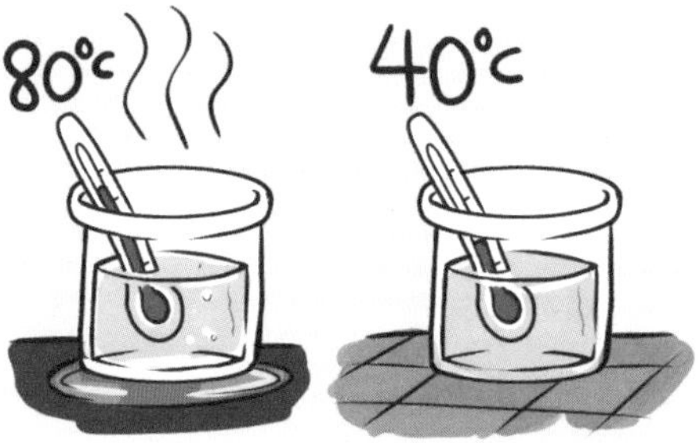
80°c
40°c

2. Mix in a tablespoon of your favourite store-bought yogurt (known as your starter culture).

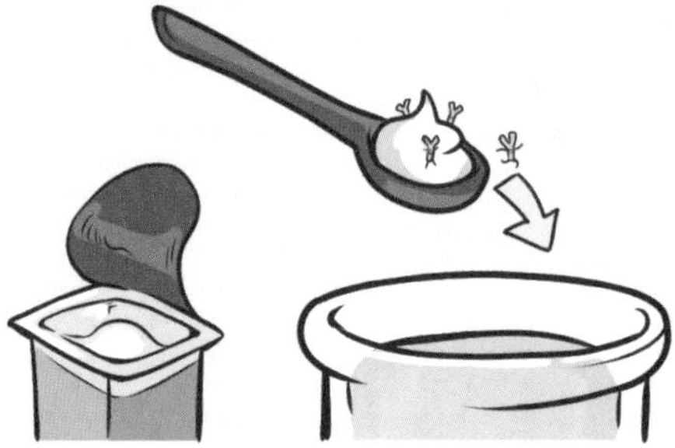

3. Cover your homemade yogurt and leave it in a warm place for 5-10 hours (for the good bacteria in the starter culture to work its magic), depending on how sour you want your yogurt to be.

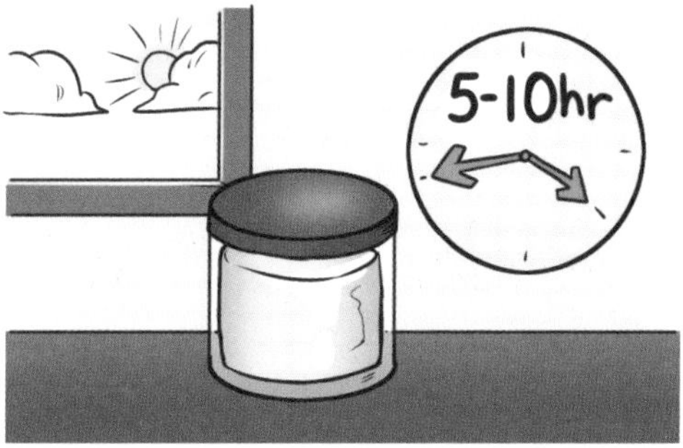
5-10hr

4. Store your homemade yogurt (which should now no longer look like milk) in the fridge and consume within 5 days for the best taste (yogurt will become more sour with time).

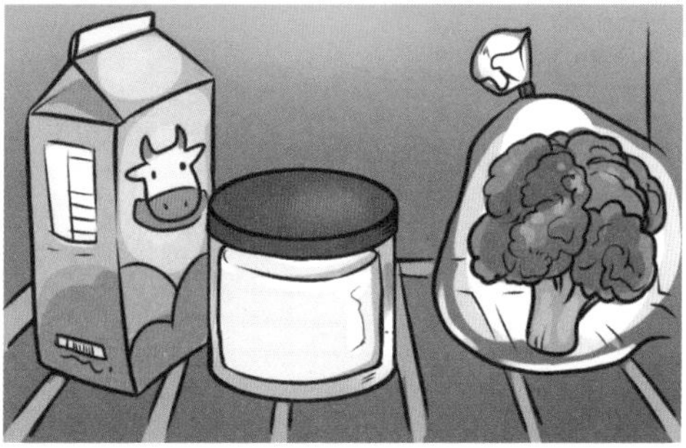

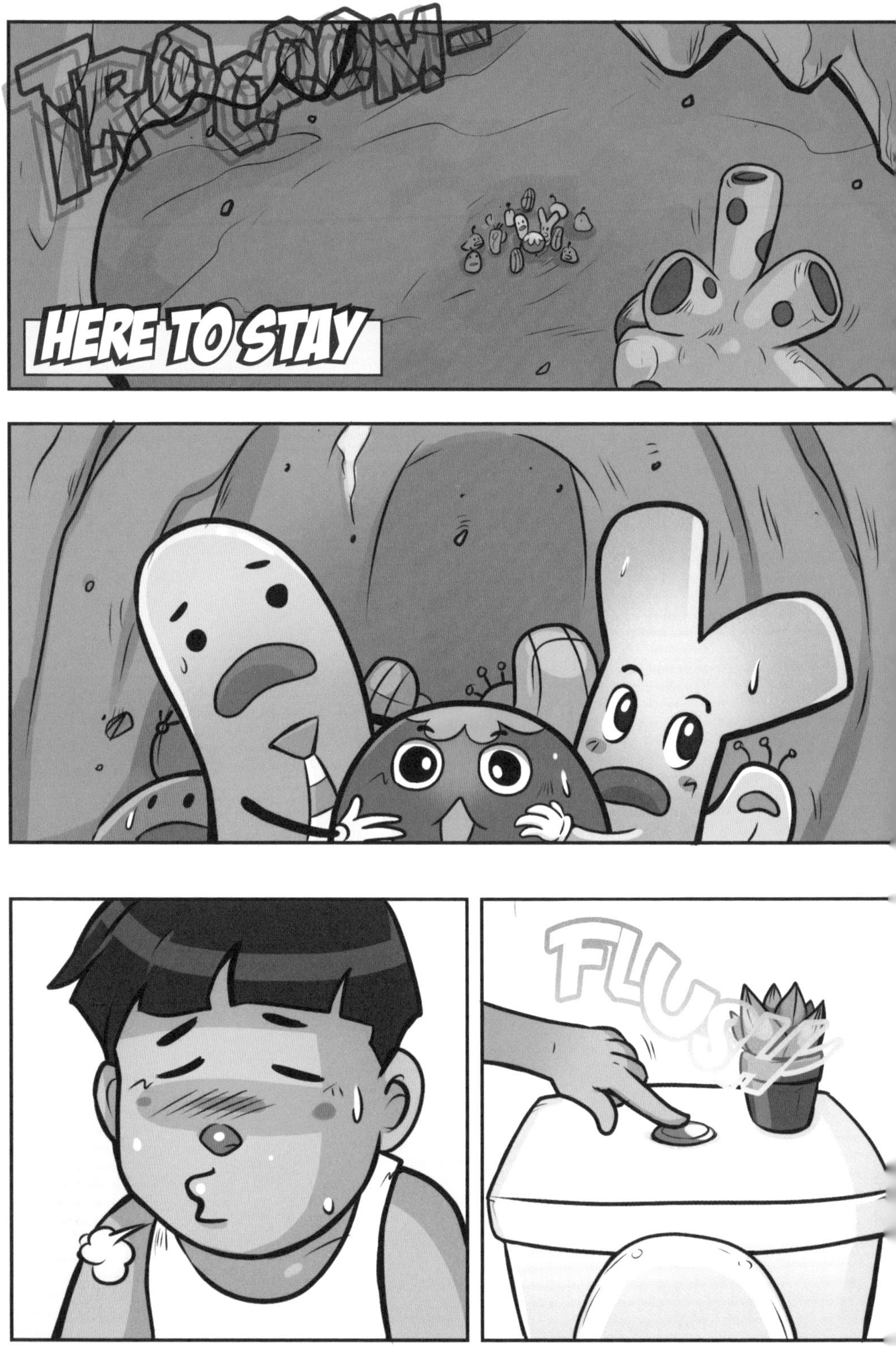
HERE TO STAY

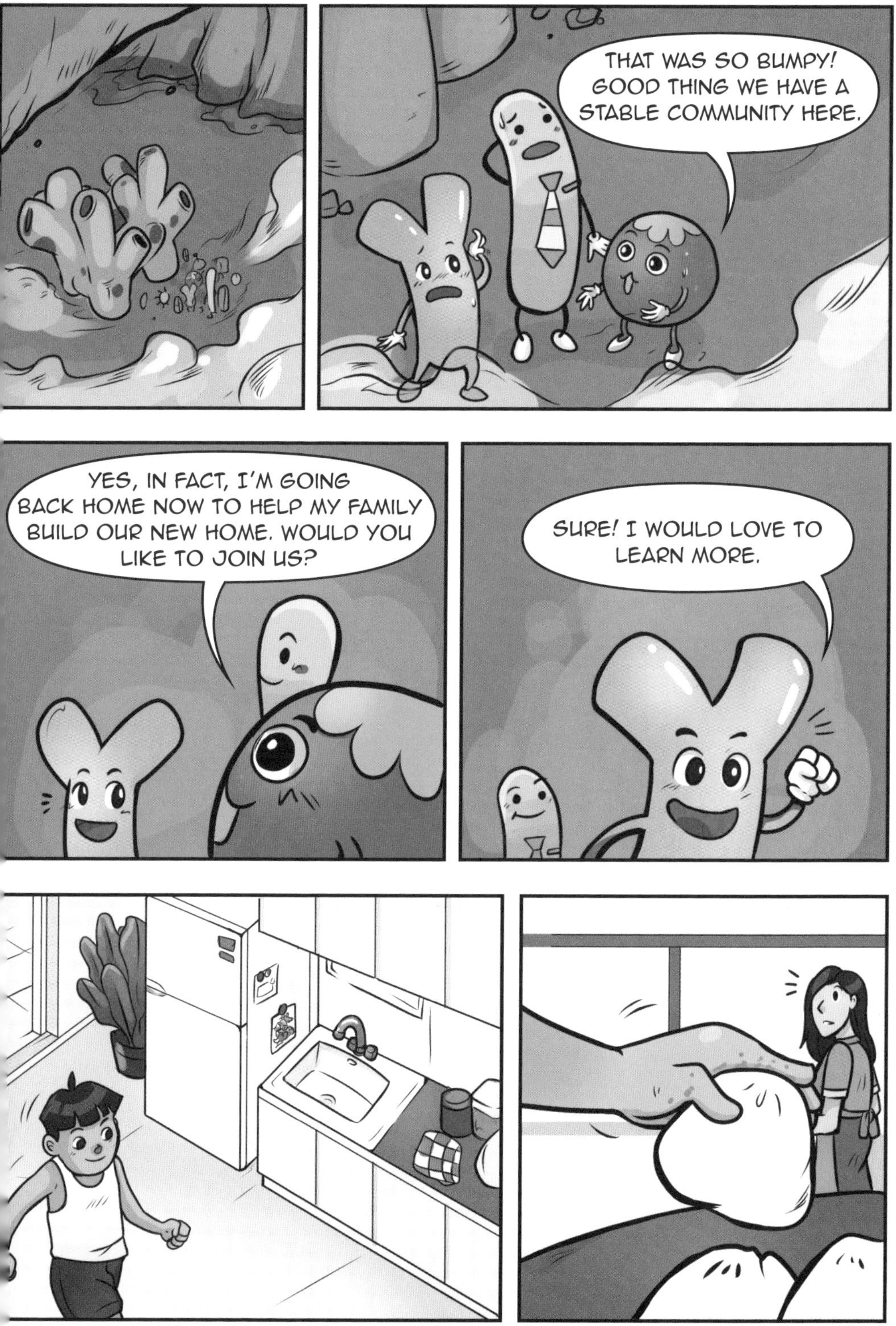
THAT WAS SO BUMPY! GOOD THING WE HAVE A STABLE COMMUNITY HERE.
YES, IN FACT, I'M GOING BACK HOME NOW TO HELP MY FAMILY BUILD OUR NEW HOME. WOULD YOU LIKE TO JOIN US?
SURE! I WOULD LOVE TO LEARN MORE.

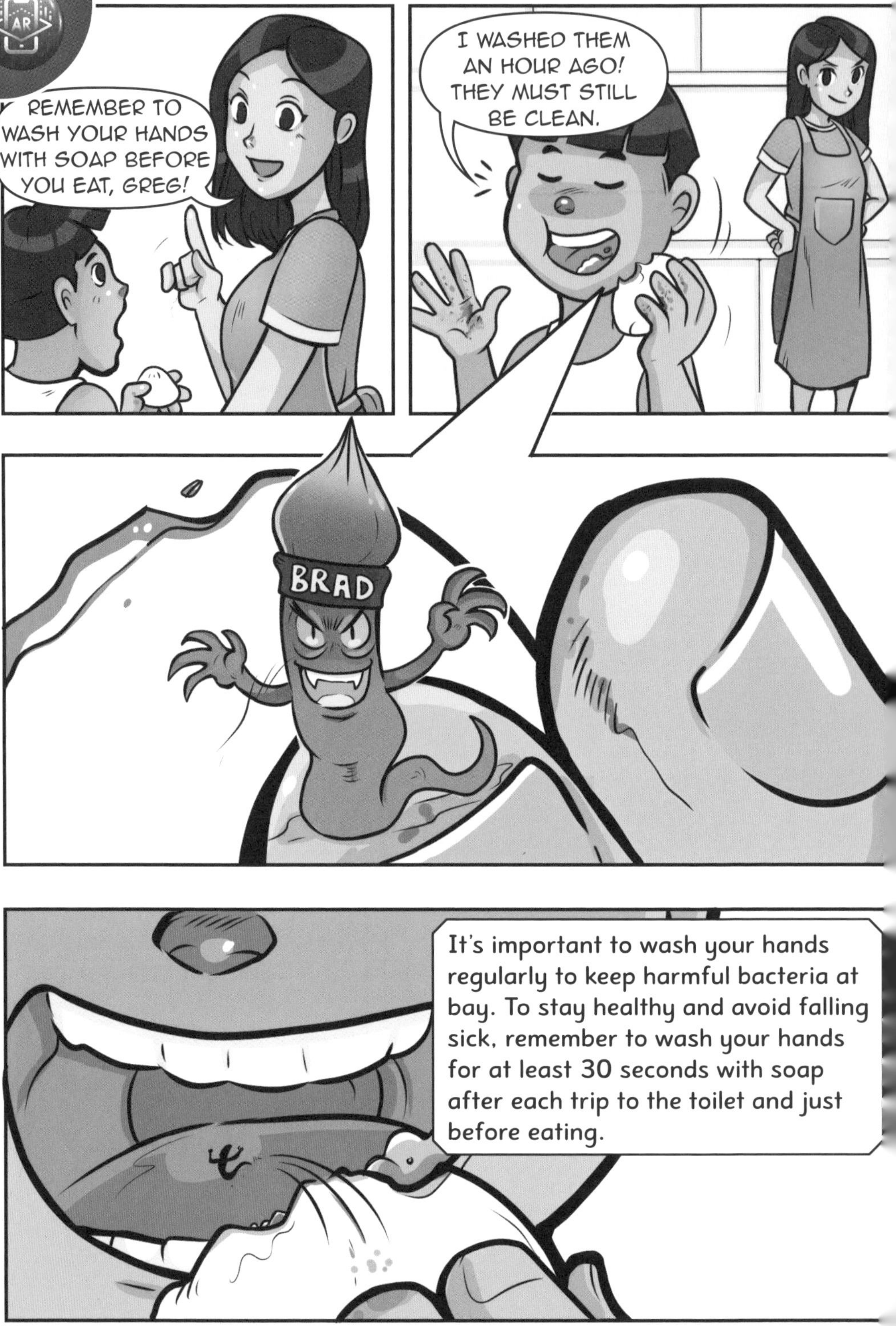
REMEMBER TO WASH YOUR HANDS WITH SOAP BEFORE YOU EAT, GREG!
I WASHED THEM AN HOUR AGO! THEY MUST STILL BE CLEAN.
BRAD
It's important to wash your hands regularly to keep harmful bacteria at bay. To stay healthy and avoid falling sick, remember to wash your hands for at least 30 seconds with soap after each trip to the toilet and just before eating.

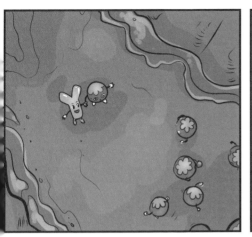

GUSS, THIS IS MY MUM.

HI AUNTIE! NICE TO MEET YOU.

GUSS IS NEW TO GREG'S GUT. I INVITED HIM OVER TO JOIN US AS WE BUILD OUR NEW HOME.

HELLO, GUSS!

THANKS FOR LETTING ME JOIN YOU.

LET'S GET TO WORK!

THE FIRST STEP IS MAKING SURE WE HAVE ENOUGH OF US TO CREATE A SIZEABLE COMMUNITY.
WE ACHIEVE THIS BY MULTIPLYING IN NUMBERS.
ONE THING THAT IS INTERESTING ABOUT US BACTERIA....
...IS THAT WE MULTIPLY BY DIVIDING!

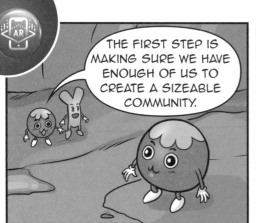

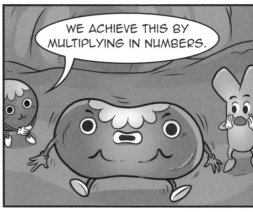

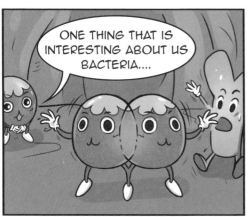

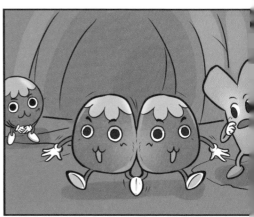

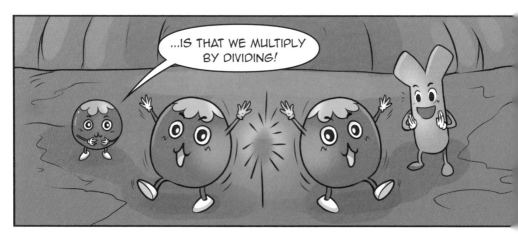

Bacteria divide by binary fission. In this process, a bacterial cell replicates its circular DNA. The 2 copies of DNA move to opposite ends of the cell and the cell divides into two identical daughter cells.

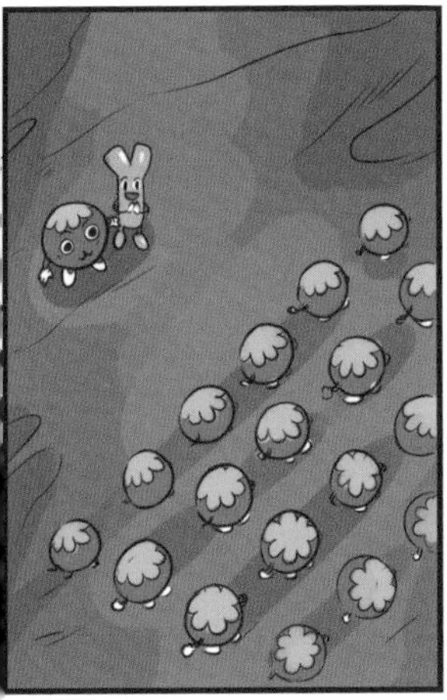

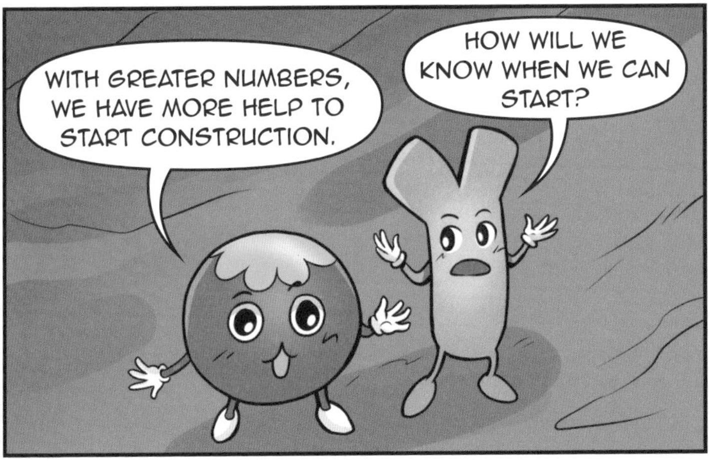
WITH GREATER NUMBERS, WE HAVE MORE HELP TO START CONSTRUCTION.
HOW WILL WE KNOW WHEN WE CAN START?

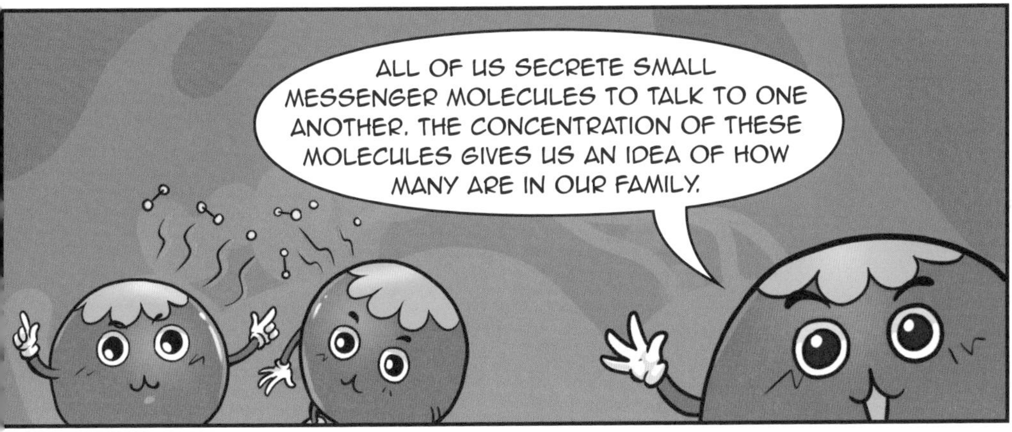
ALL OF US SECRETE SMALL MESSENGER MOLECULES TO TALK TO ONE ANOTHER. THE CONCENTRATION OF THESE MOLECULES GIVES US AN IDEA OF HOW MANY ARE IN OUR FAMILY.

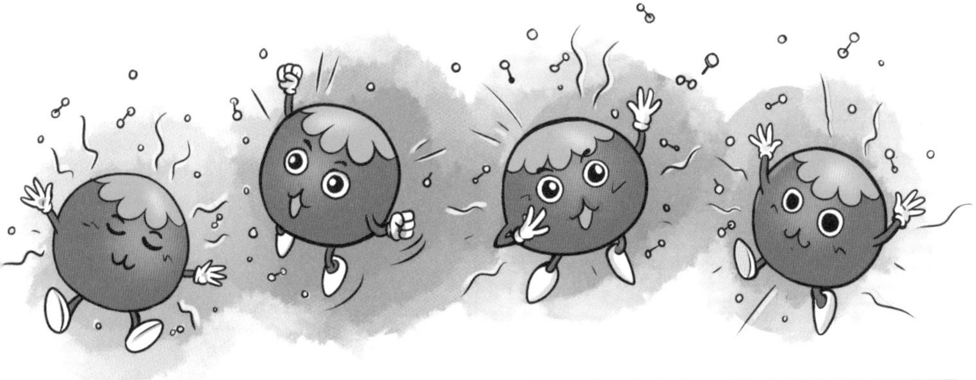

Bacteria communicate with one another through simple small molecules, which vary in concentration depending on the number of bacteria and message being conveyed. This process of sensing and communicating with fellow bacteria is known as quorum sensing.

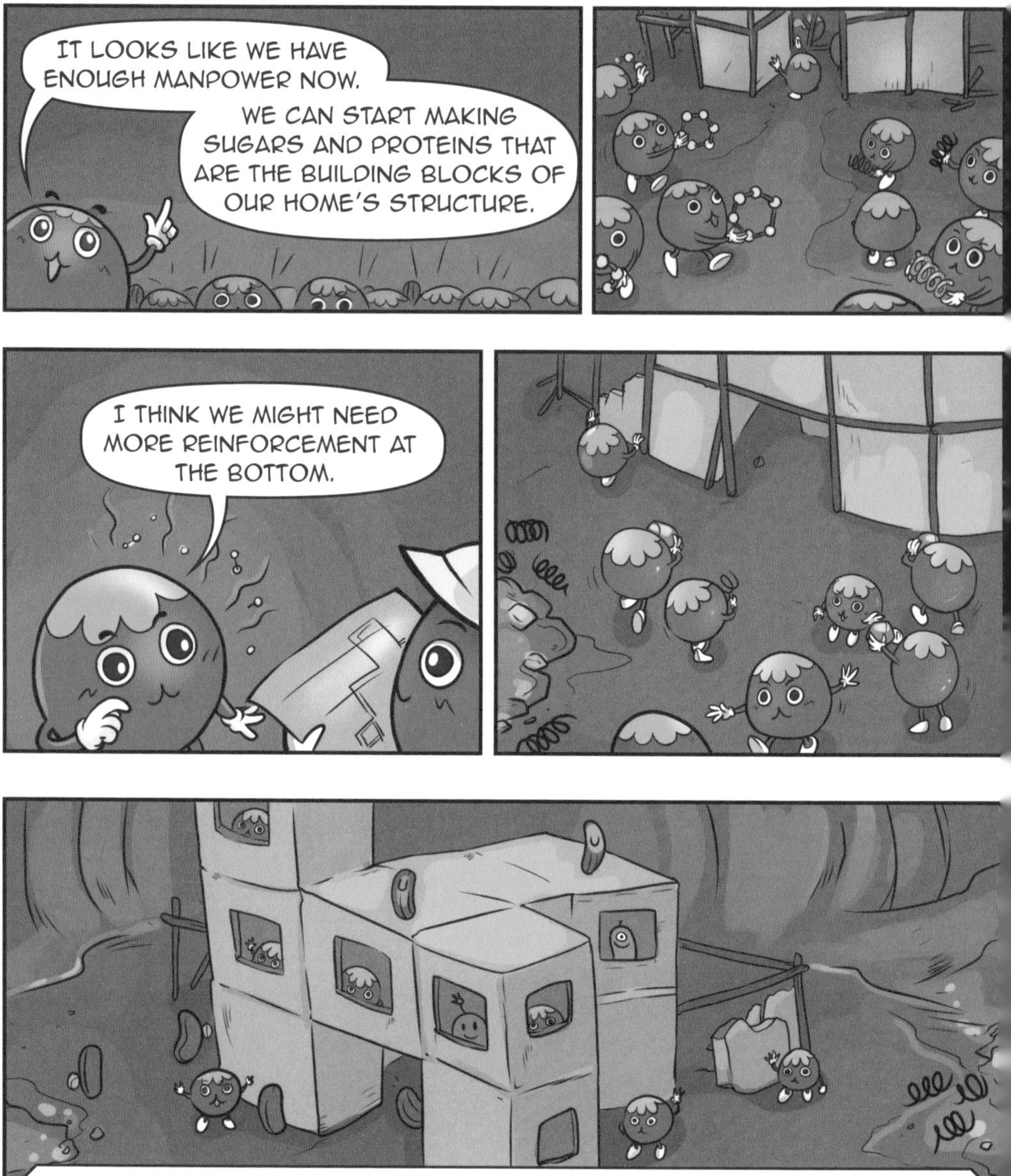
IT LOOKS LIKE WE HAVE ENOUGH MANPOWER NOW.
WE CAN START MAKING SUGARS AND PROTEINS THAT ARE THE BUILDING BLOCKS OF OUR HOME'S STRUCTURE.
I THINK WE MIGHT NEED MORE REINFORCEMENT AT THE BOTTOM.

As compared to a planktonic lifestyle where individual bacteria are free to roam about, bacteria behave very differently when they settle down as a community into a fixed home called a biofilm. The biofilm is made up of different types of building blocks that contribute to the unique lifestyle of bacteria in biofilms, including increased resilience to being washed away or harmed by antibiotics. This can be good for Greg if good bacteria form biofilms, but can also pose threats to Greg's health if bad bacteria manage to start establishing biofilm communities.

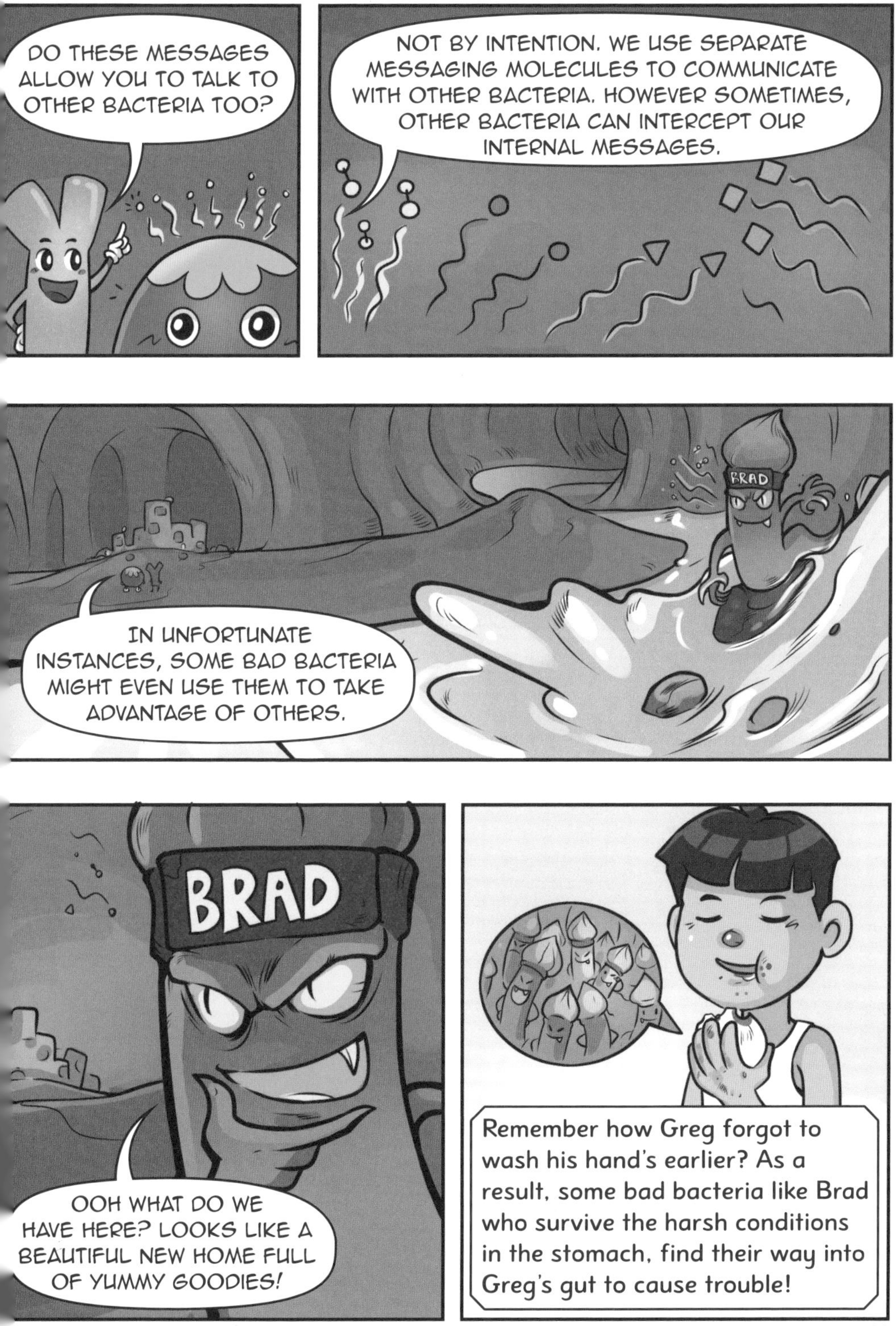
DO THESE MESSAGES ALLOW YOU TO TALK TO OTHER BACTERIA TOO?
NOT BY INTENTION. WE USE SEPARATE MESSAGING MOLECULES TO COMMUNICATE WITH OTHER BACTERIA. HOWEVER SOMETIMES, OTHER BACTERIA CAN INTERCEPT OUR INTERNAL MESSAGES.
BRAD
IN UNFORTUNATE INSTANCES, SOME BAD BACTERIA MIGHT EVEN USE THEM TO TAKE ADVANTAGE OF OTHERS.
BRAD
OOH WHAT DO WE HAVE HERE? LOOKS LIKE A BEAUTIFUL NEW HOME FULL OF YUMMY GOODIES!
Remember how Greg forgot to wash his hand's earlier? As a result, some bad bacteria like Brad who survive the harsh conditions in the stomach, find their way into Greg's gut to cause trouble!

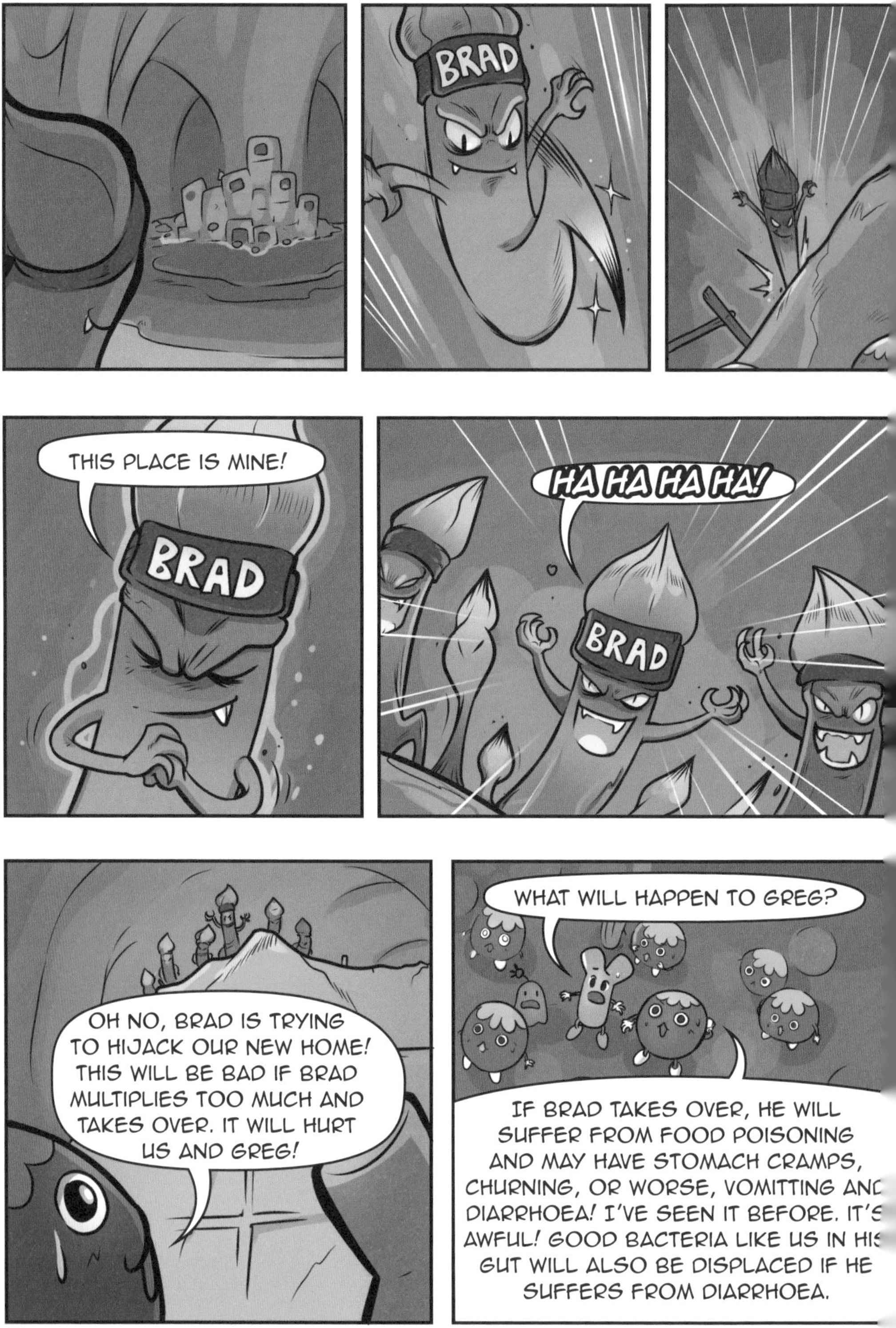
BRAD
BRAD
THIS PLACE IS MINE!
BRAD
HA HA HA HA!
BRAD
OH NO, BRAD IS TRYING TO HIJACK OUR NEW HOME! THIS WILL BE BAD IF BRAD MULTIPLIES TOO MUCH AND TAKES OVER. IT WILL HURT US AND GREG!
WHAT WILL HAPPEN TO GREG?
IF BRAD TAKES OVER, HE WILL SUFFER FROM FOOD POISONING AND MAY HAVE STOMACH CRAMPS, CHURNING, OR WORSE, VOMITTING AND DIARRHOEA! I'VE SEEN IT BEFORE. IT'S AWFUL! GOOD BACTERIA LIKE US IN HIS GUT WILL ALSO BE DISPLACED IF HE SUFFERS FROM DIARRHOEA.

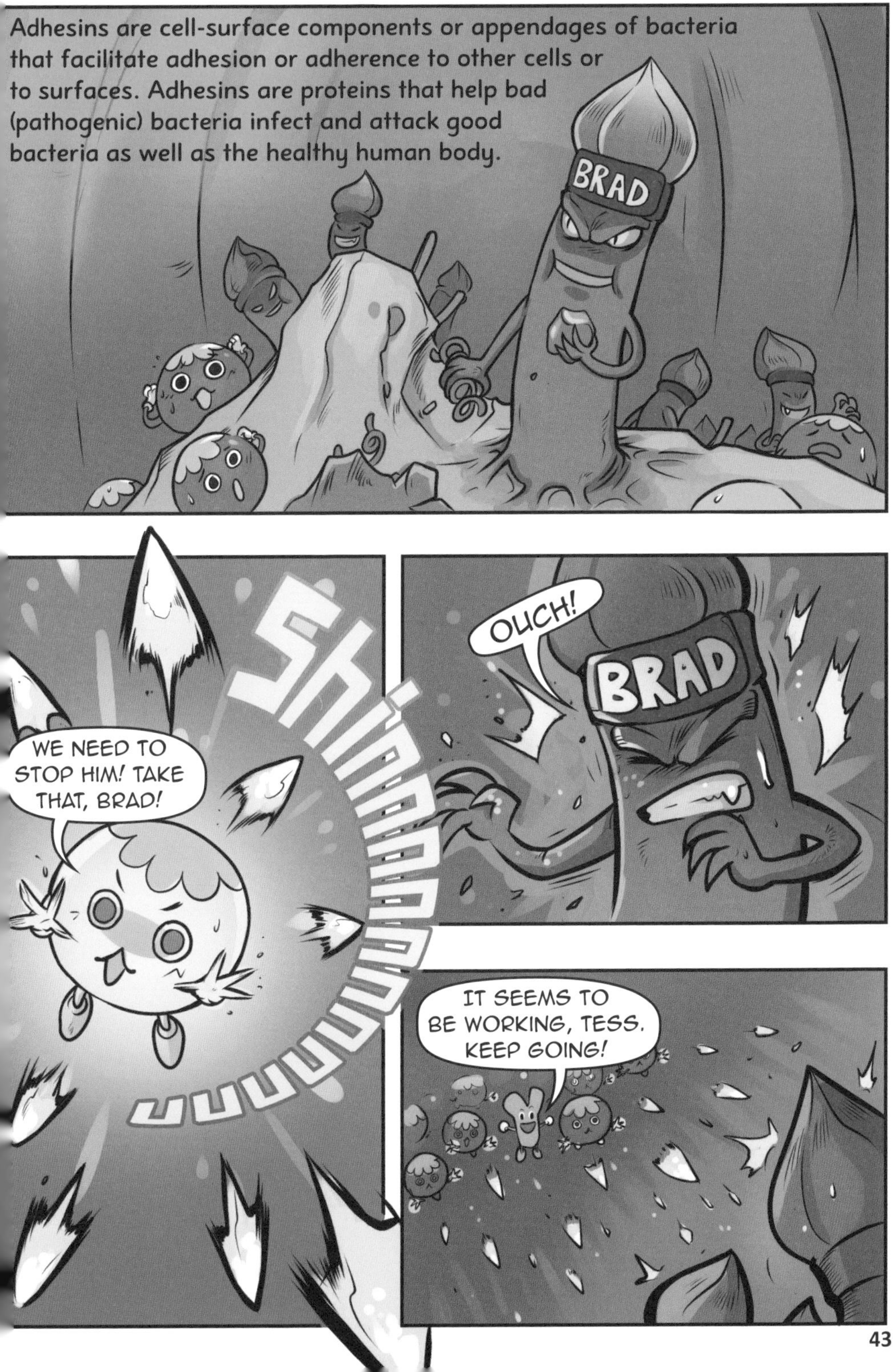
Adhesins are cell-surface components or appendages of bacteria that facilitate adhesion or adherence to other cells or to surfaces. Adhesins are proteins that help bad (pathogenic) bacteria infect and attack good bacteria as well as the healthy human body.
BRAD
WE NEED TO STOP HIM! TAKE THAT, BRAD!
OUCH!
BRAD
IT SEEMS TO BE WORKING, TESS. KEEP GOING!

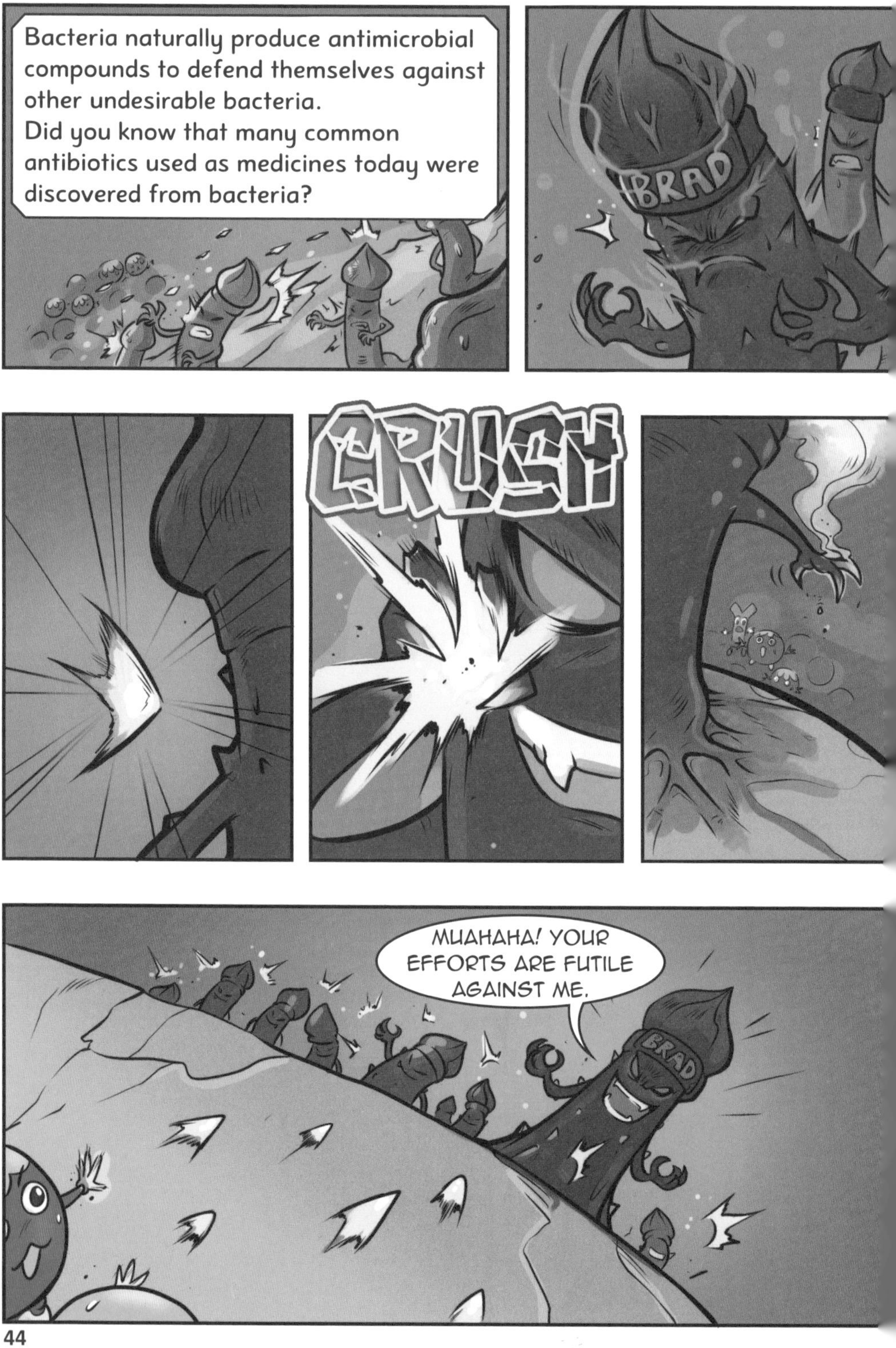
Bacteria naturally produce antimicrobial compounds to defend themselves against other undesirable bacteria.
Did you know that many common antibiotics used as medicines today were discovered from bacteria?
BRAD
CRUSH
MUAHAHA! YOUR EFFORTS ARE FUTILE AGAINST ME.
BRAD

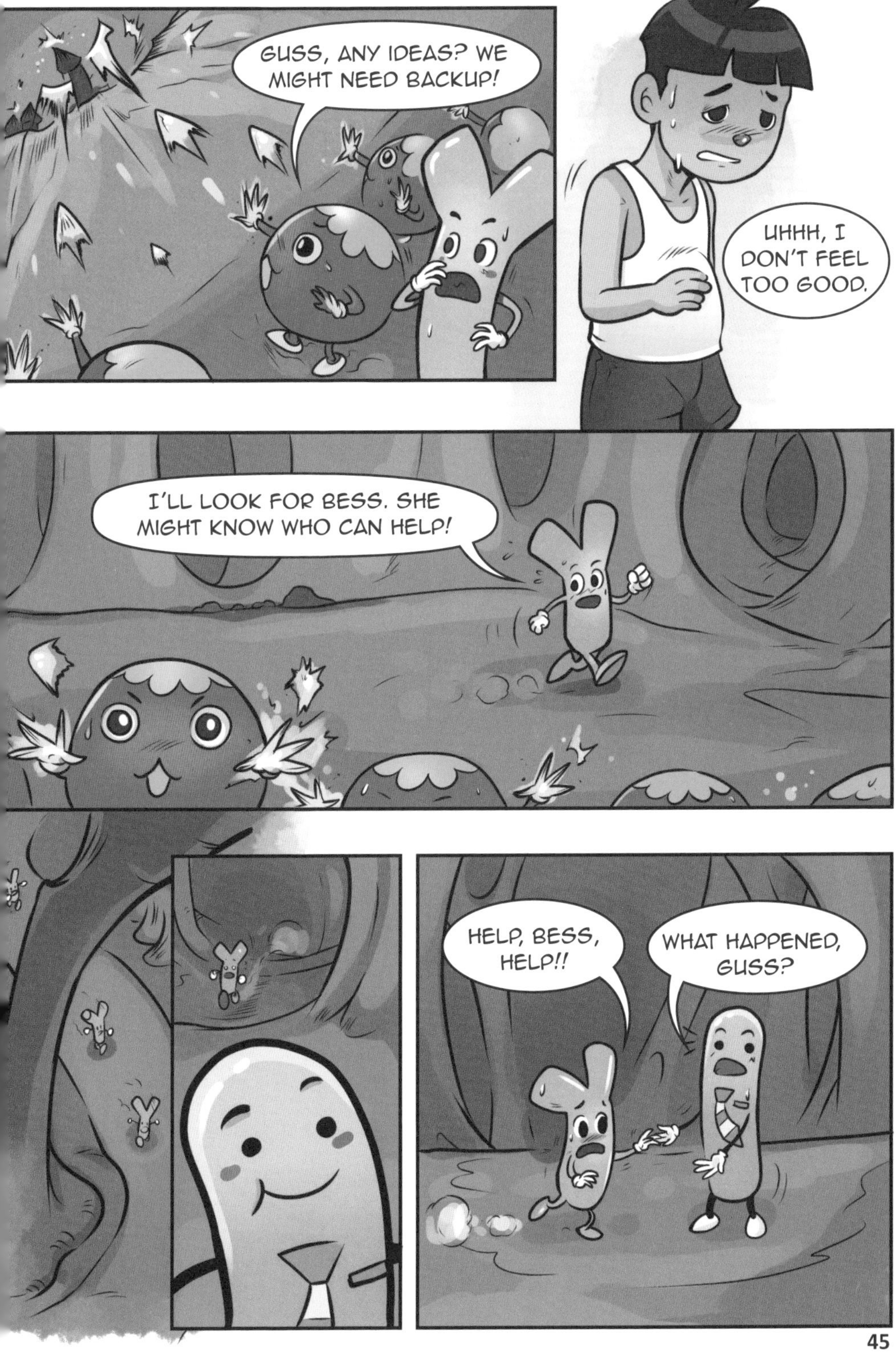
GUSS, ANY IDEAS? WE MIGHT NEED BACKUP!
UHHH, I DON'T FEEL TOO GOOD.
I'LL LOOK FOR BESS. SHE MIGHT KNOW WHO CAN HELP!
HELP, BESS, HELP!!
WHAT HAPPENED, GUSS?

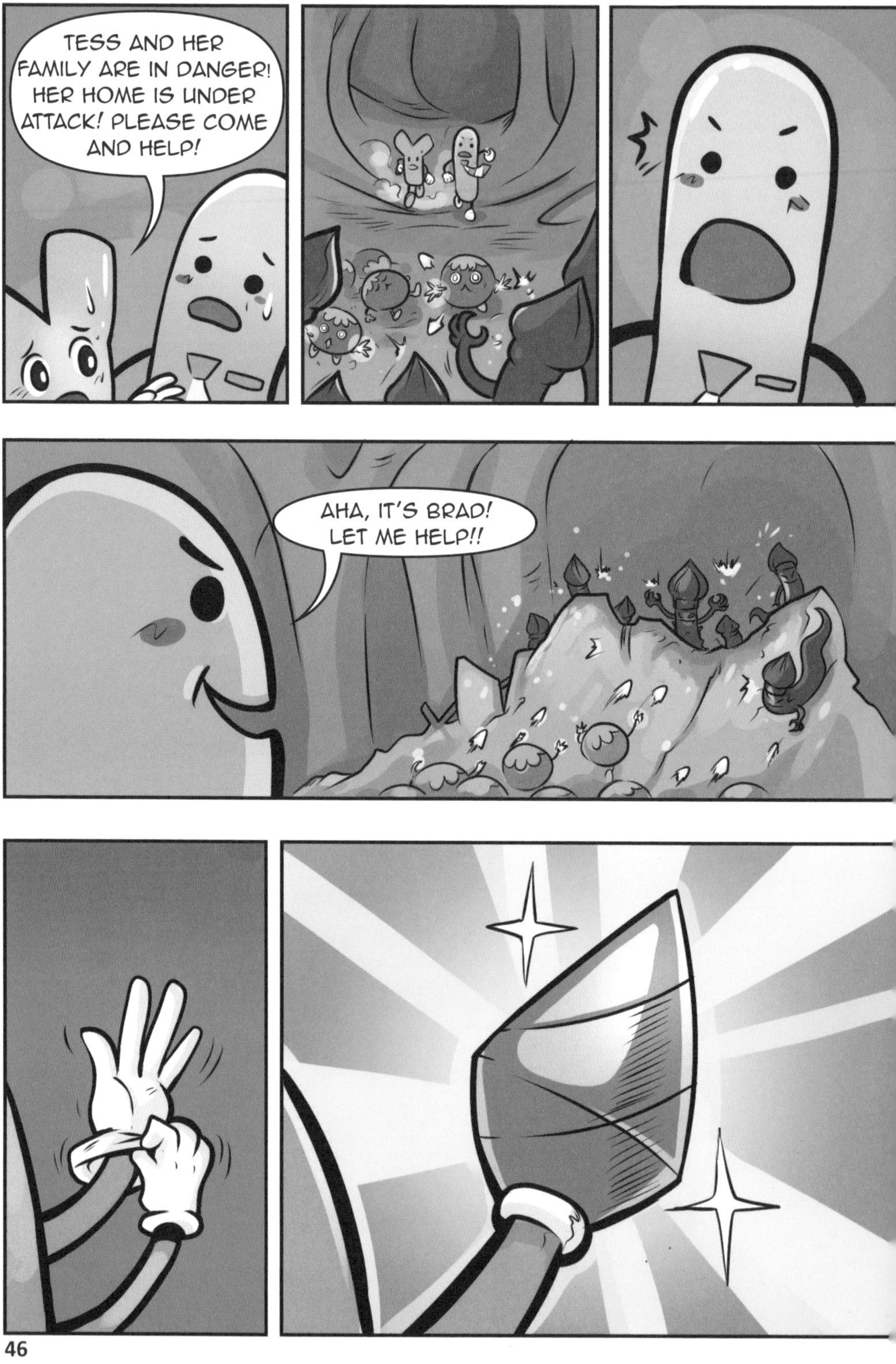
TESS AND HER FAMILY ARE IN DANGER! HER HOME IS UNDER ATTACK! PLEASE COME AND HELP!
AHA, IT'S BRAD! LET ME HELP!!

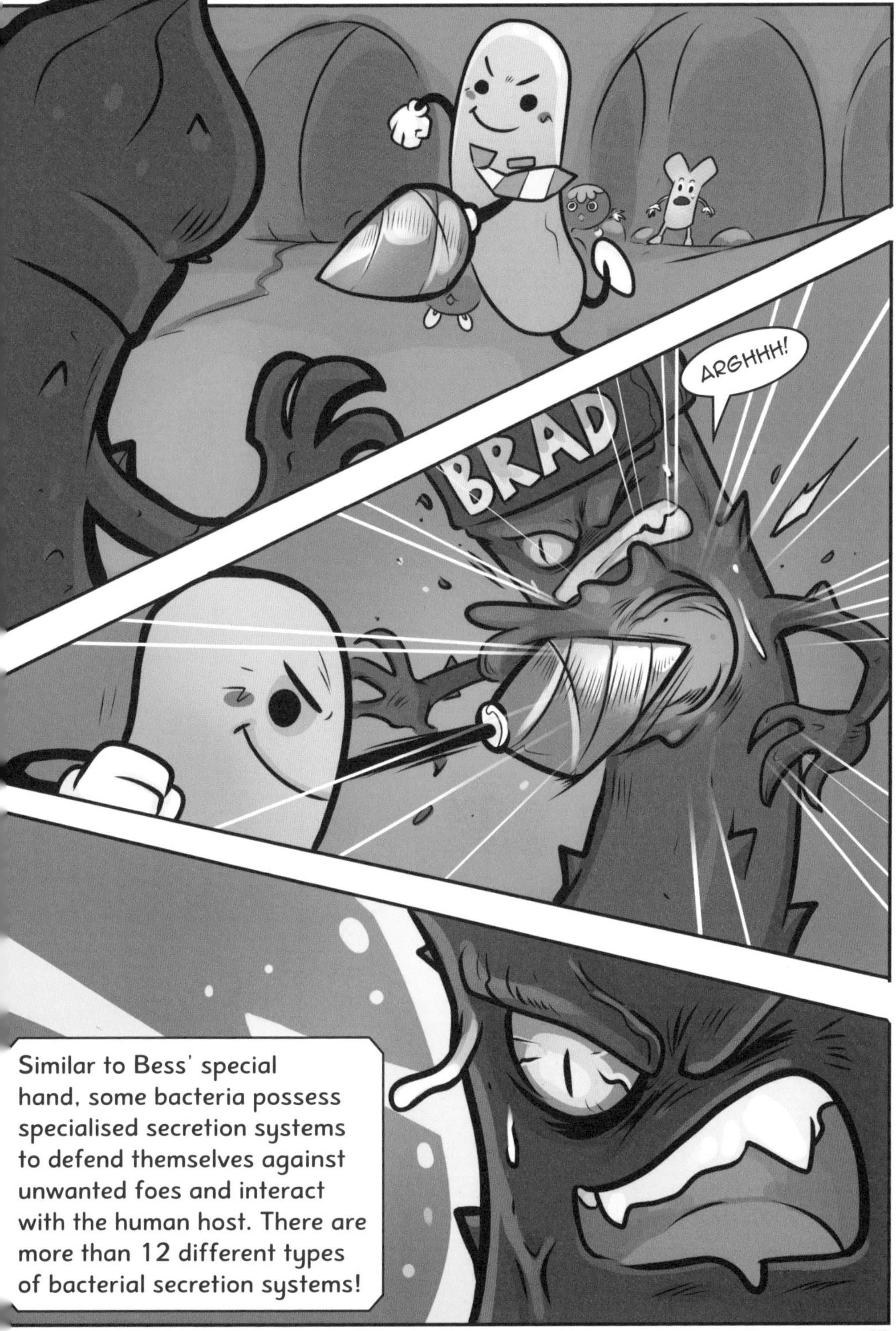
ARGHHH!
BRAD
Similar to Bess' special hand, some bacteria possess specialised secretion systems to defend themselves against unwanted foes and interact with the human host. There are more than 12 different types of bacterial secretion systems!

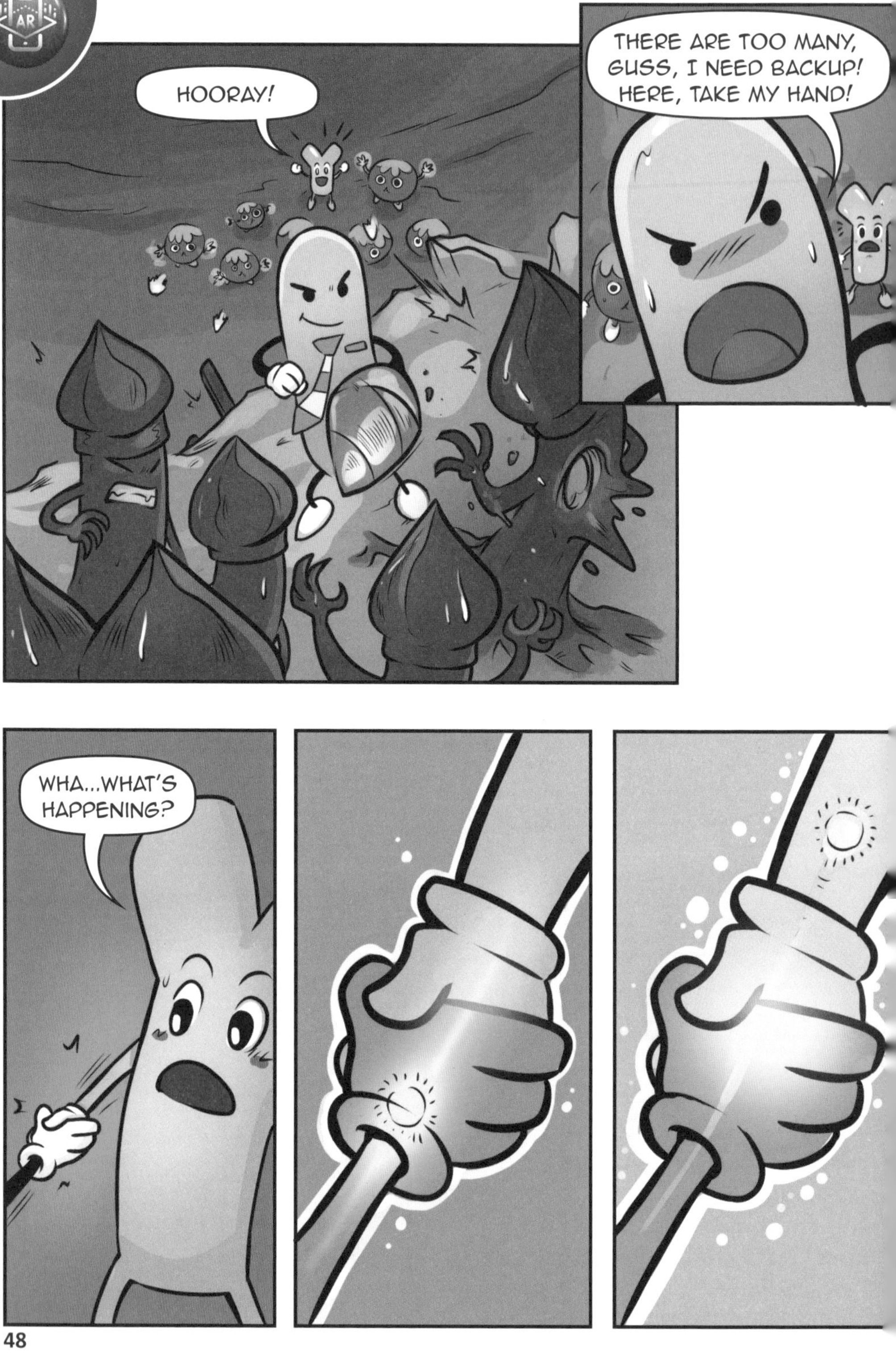
HOORAY!
THERE ARE TOO MANY, GUSS, I NEED BACKUP! HERE, TAKE MY HAND!
WHA...WHAT'S HAPPENING?

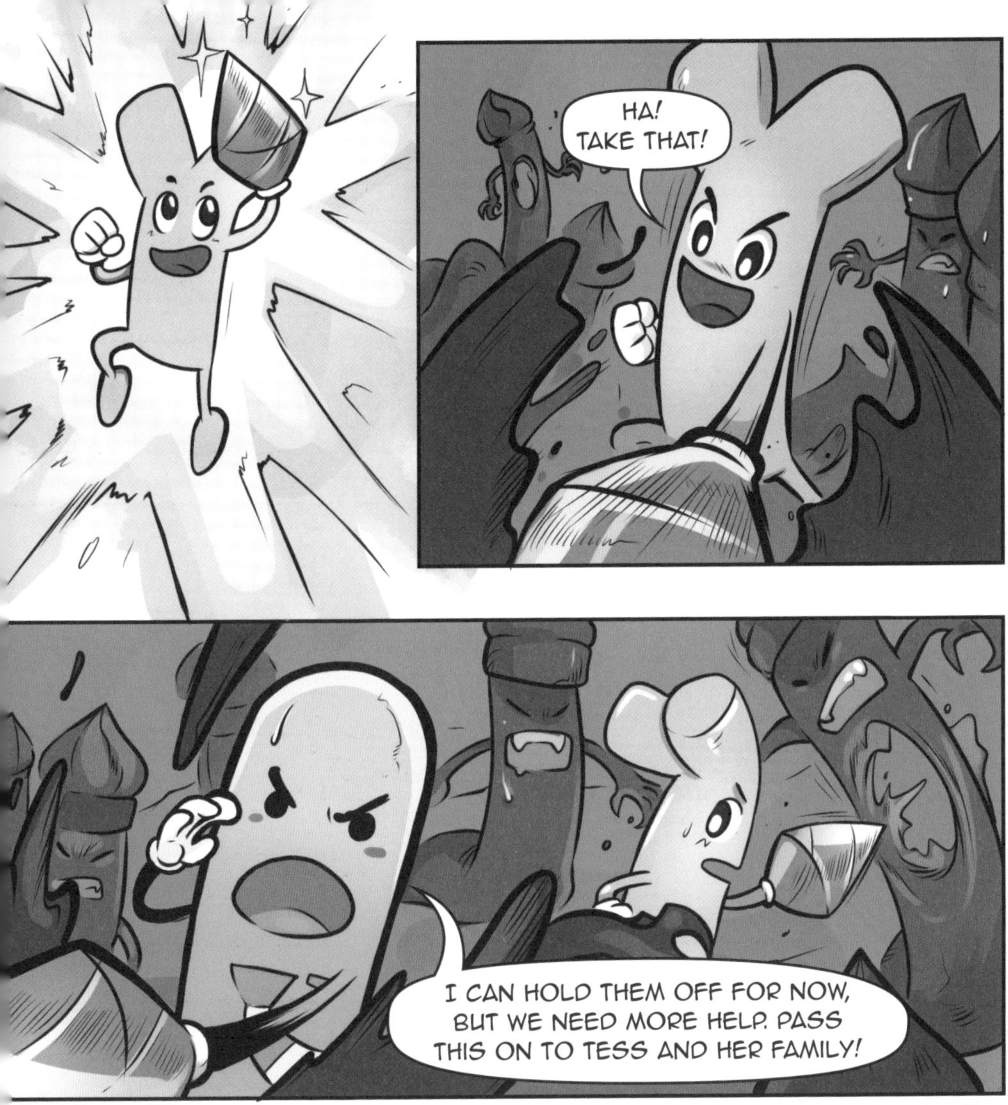
HA! TAKE THAT!
I CAN HOLD THEM OFF FOR NOW, BUT WE NEED MORE HELP. PASS THIS ON TO TESS AND HER FAMILY!

Bacteria share genetic material called DNA with one another all the time, which convey instructions on how to perform specific tasks such as make proteins and sugars. One common mechanism to transfer such informative DNA between donor and recipient bacteria is conjugation, which is how Bess successfully shares her ability to defend against Brad with Guss.

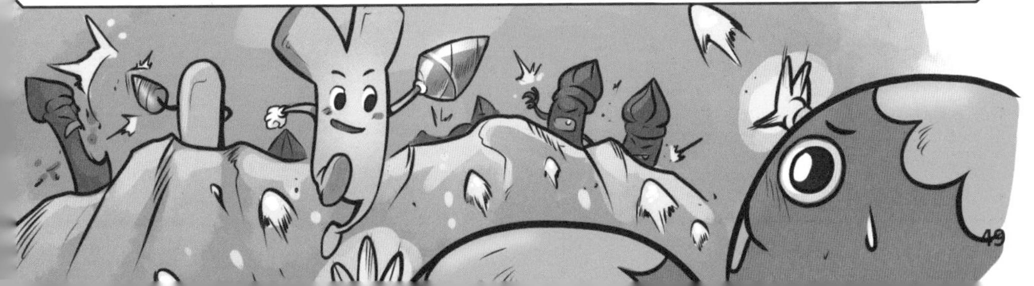

HURRY, TESS! TAKE MY HAND!
THIS IS FROM BESS. SHE'S HOLDING OFF BRAD FOR NOW BUT NEEDS MORE HELP.
THANK YOU GUSS! YOU AND BESS ARE LIFESAVERS.
TAKE THAT!

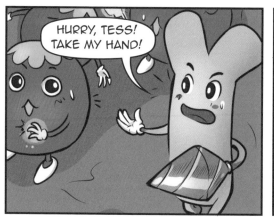

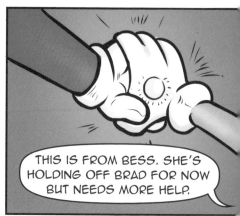

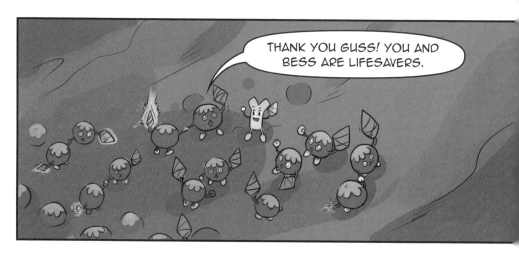

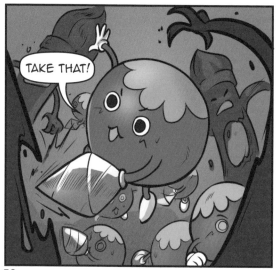

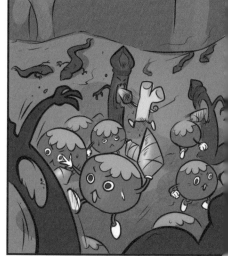

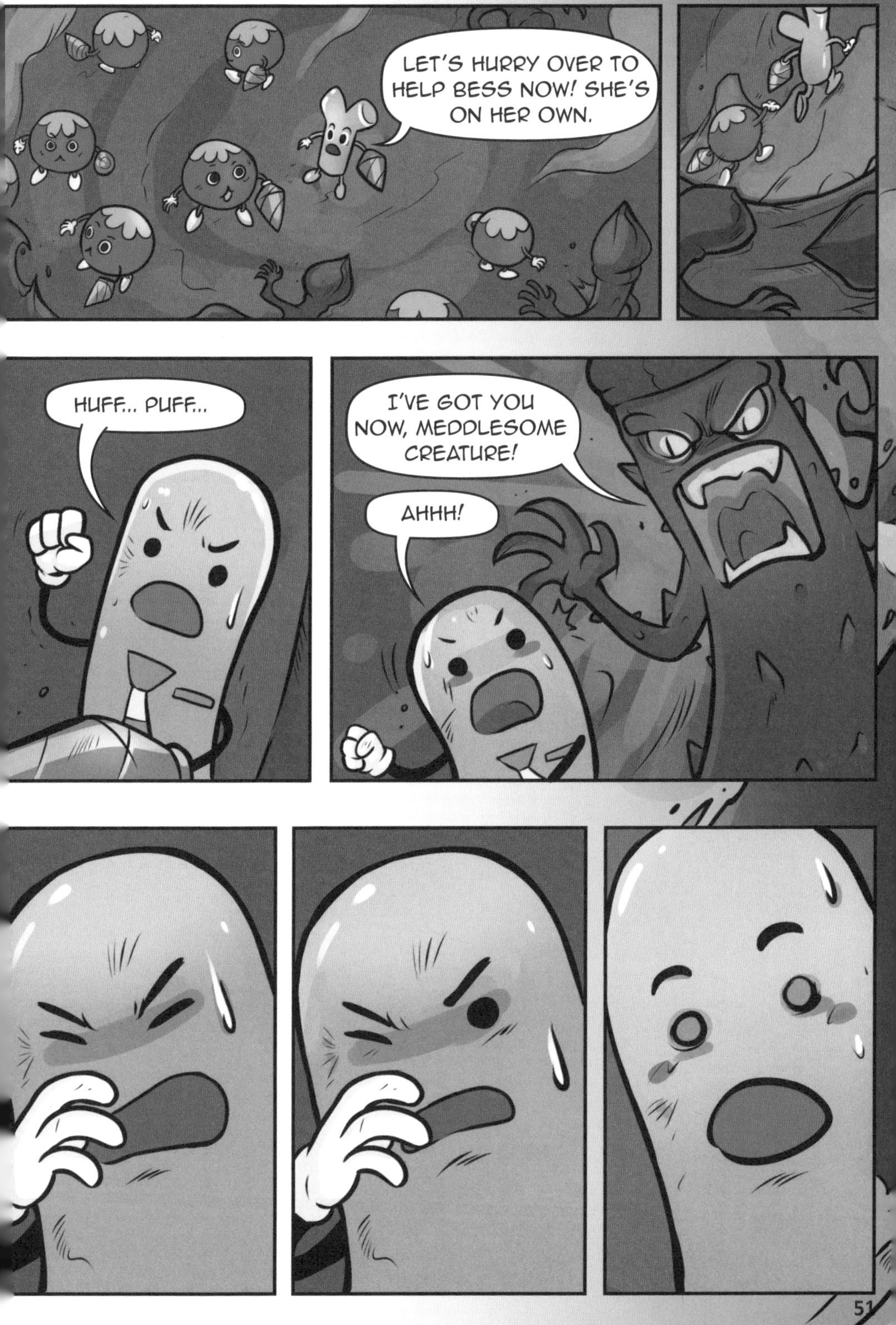
LET'S HURRY OVER TO HELP BESS NOW! SHE'S ON HER OWN.
HUFF... PUFF...
I'VE GOT YOU NOW, MEDDLESOME CREATURE!
AHHH!

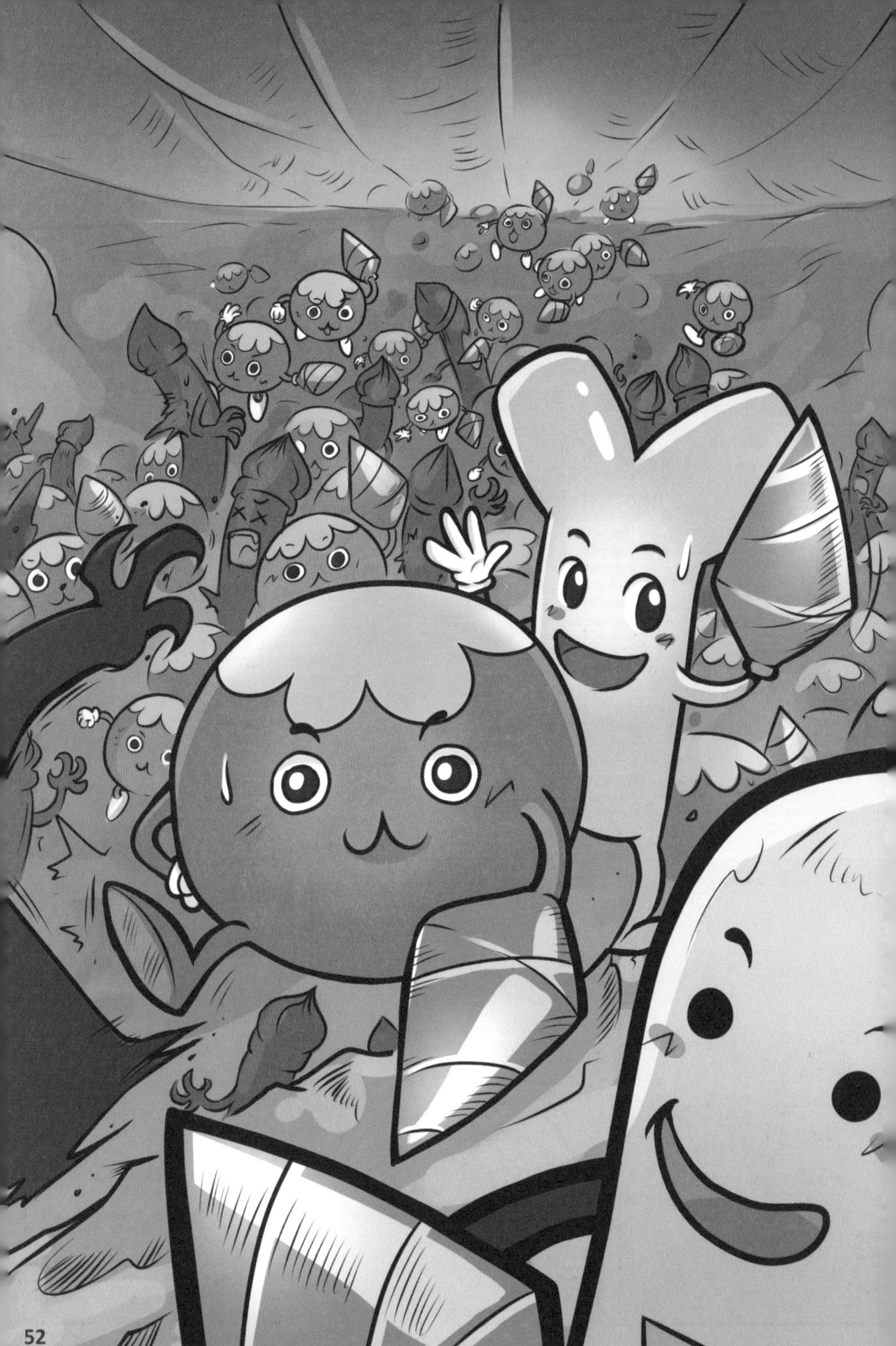

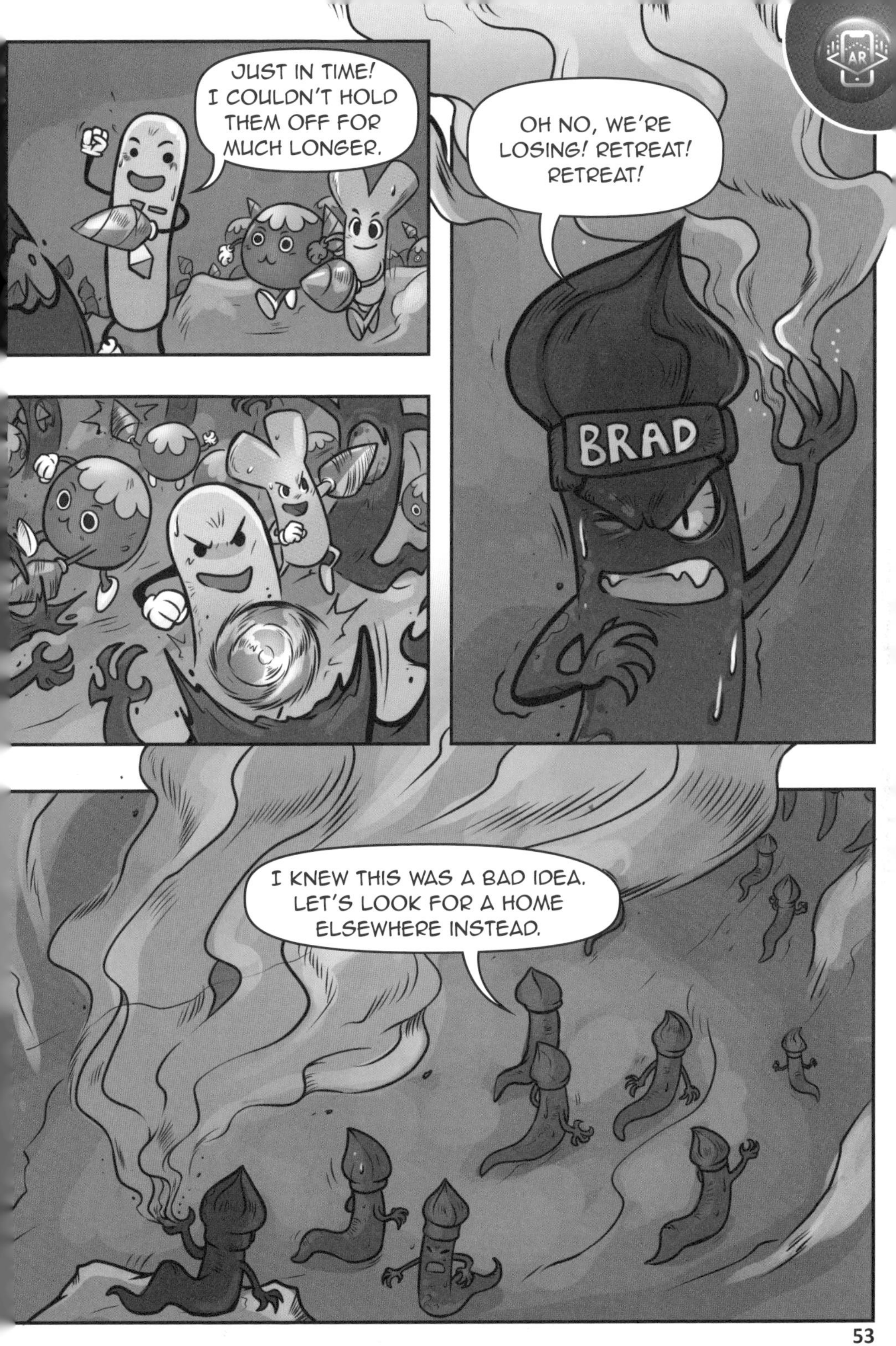
JUST IN TIME! I COULDN'T HOLD THEM OFF FOR MUCH LONGER.
OH NO, WE'RE LOSING! RETREAT! RETREAT!
BRAD
I KNEW THIS WAS A BAD IDEA. LET'S LOOK FOR A HOME ELSEWHERE INSTEAD.

It's very busy in the gut. Apart from learning to co-exist, good bacteria in the gut also need to learn how to defend their homes against bad bacteria for survival and to keep you healthy. Taking antibiotics unnecessarily can harm your good bacteria and leave them more vulnerable to attack by bad bacteria.

Many bad bacteria can co-exist in our gut in controlled numbers, and are called opportunistic pathogens because they only cause harm if left unchecked by our immune system. People with weaker immune systems (e.g., young children, elderly, pregnant women and chemotherapy patients) might have more challenges in keeping opportunistic pathogens at bay, so they need to be extra careful.

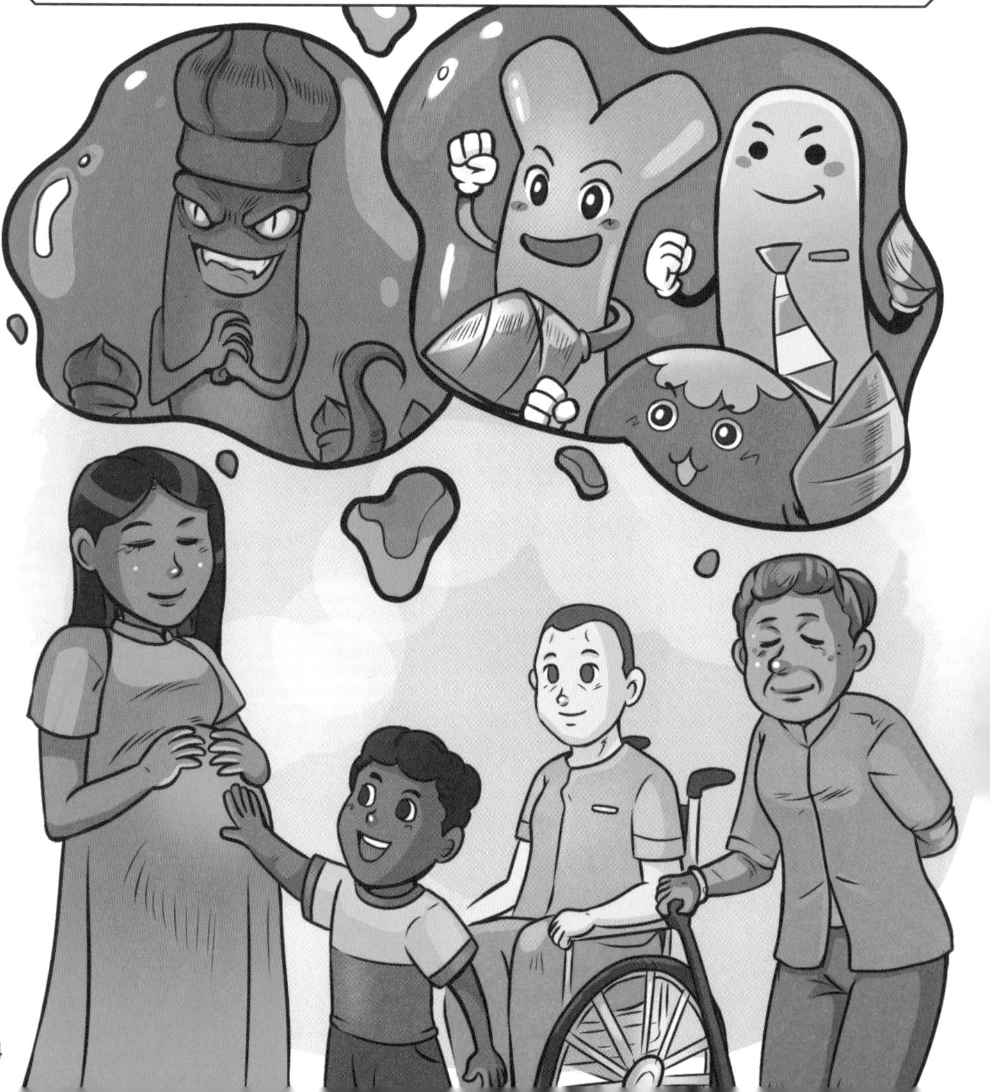

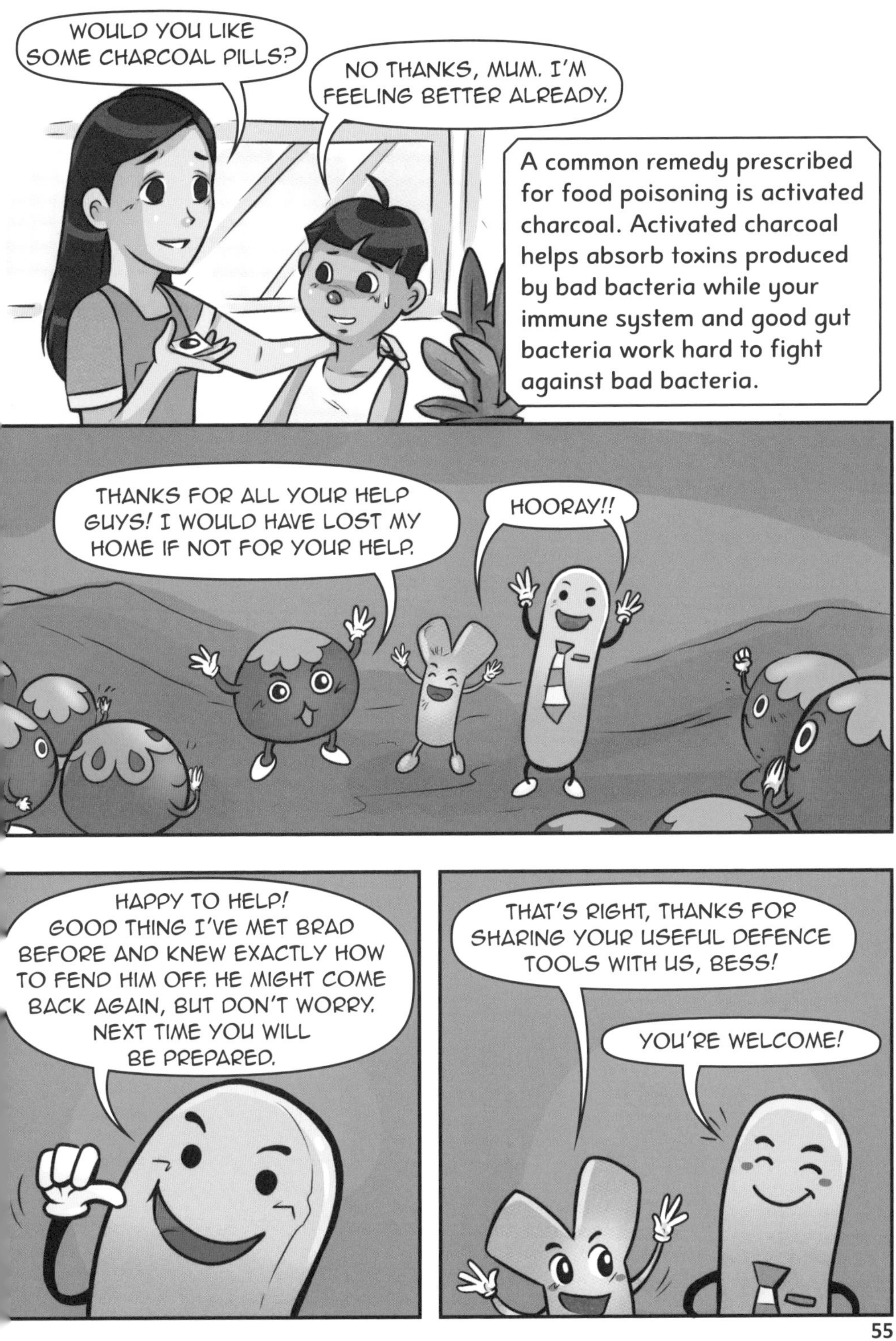

WOULD YOU LIKE SOME CHARCOAL PILLS?
NO THANKS, MUM. I'M FEELING BETTER ALREADY.
A common remedy prescribed for food poisoning is activated charcoal. Activated charcoal helps absorb toxins produced by bad bacteria while your immune system and good gut bacteria work hard to fight against bad bacteria.
THANKS FOR ALL YOUR HELP GUYS! I WOULD HAVE LOST MY HOME IF NOT FOR YOUR HELP.
HOORAY!!
HAPPY TO HELP! GOOD THING I'VE MET BRAD BEFORE AND KNEW EXACTLY HOW TO FEND HIM OFF. HE MIGHT COME BACK AGAIN, BUT DON'T WORRY. NEXT TIME YOU WILL BE PREPARED.
THAT'S RIGHT, THANKS FOR SHARING YOUR USEFUL DEFENCE TOOLS WITH US, BESS!
YOU'RE WELCOME!

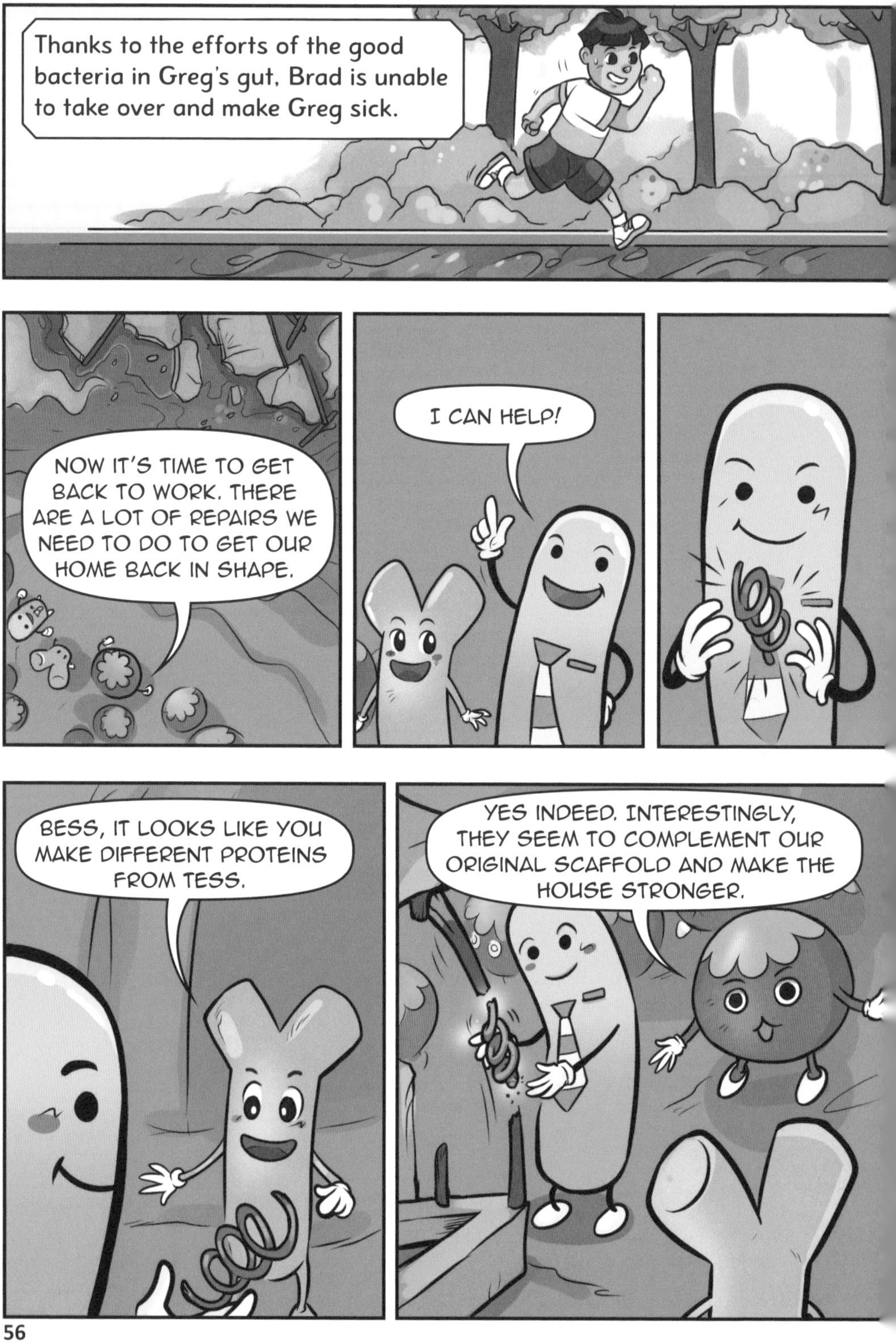
Thanks to the efforts of the good bacteria in Greg's gut, Brad is unable to take over and make Greg sick.
NOW IT'S TIME TO GET BACK TO WORK. THERE ARE A LOT OF REPAIRS WE NEED TO DO TO GET OUR HOME BACK IN SHAPE.
I CAN HELP!
BESS, IT LOOKS LIKE YOU MAKE DIFFERENT PROTEINS FROM TESS.
YES INDEED. INTERESTINGLY, THEY SEEM TO COMPLEMENT OUR ORIGINAL SCAFFOLD AND MAKE THE HOUSE STRONGER.

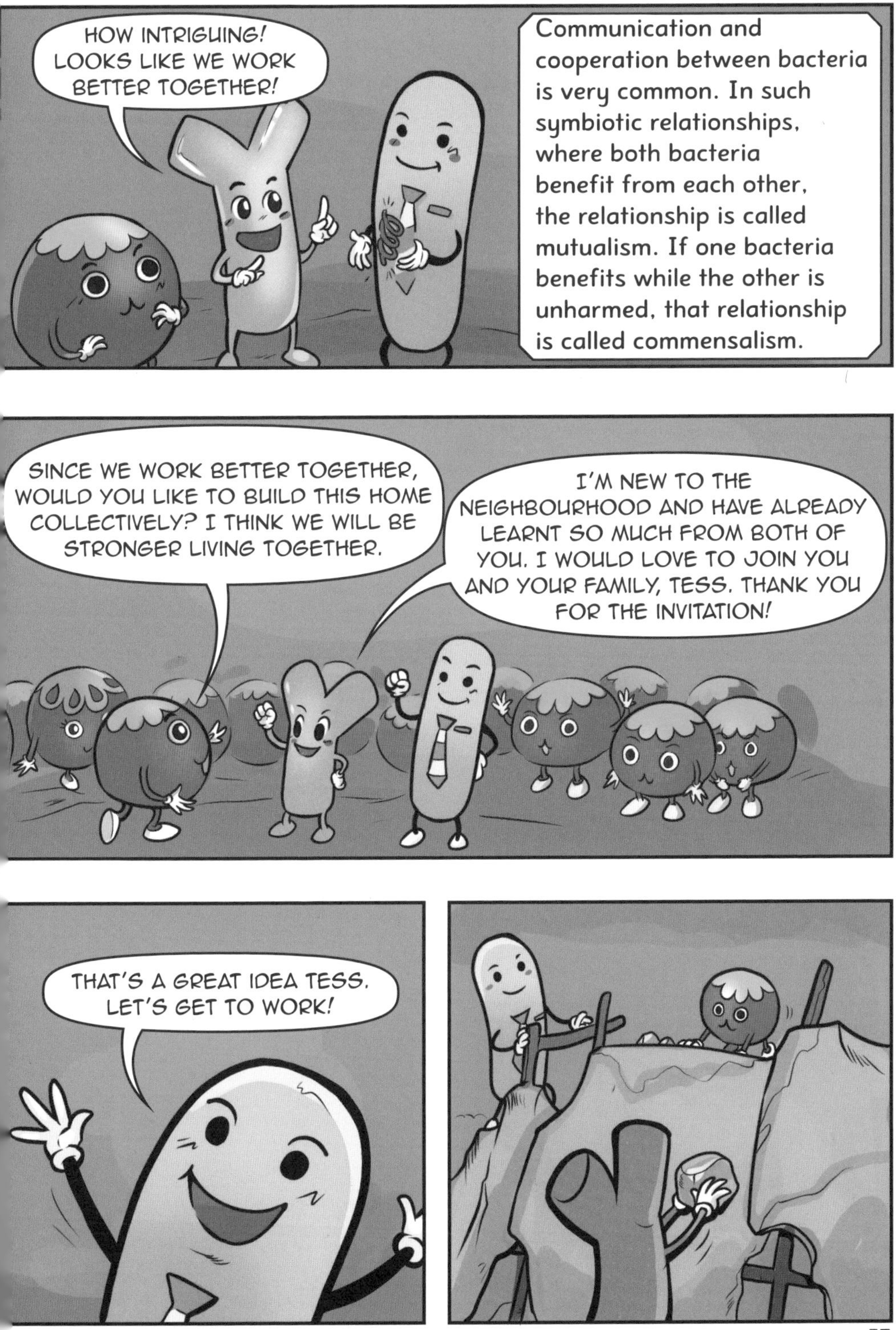
HOW INTRIGUING! LOOKS LIKE WE WORK BETTER TOGETHER!
Communication and cooperation between bacteria is very common. In such symbiotic relationships, where both bacteria benefit from each other, the relationship is called mutualism. If one bacteria benefits while the other is unharmed, that relationship is called commensalism.
SINCE WE WORK BETTER TOGETHER, WOULD YOU LIKE TO BUILD THIS HOME COLLECTIVELY? I THINK WE WILL BE STRONGER LIVING TOGETHER.
I'M NEW TO THE NEIGHBOURHOOD AND HAVE ALREADY LEARNT SO MUCH FROM BOTH OF YOU. I WOULD LOVE TO JOIN YOU AND YOUR FAMILY, TESS. THANK YOU FOR THE INVITATION!
THAT'S A GREAT IDEA TESS. LET'S GET TO WORK!

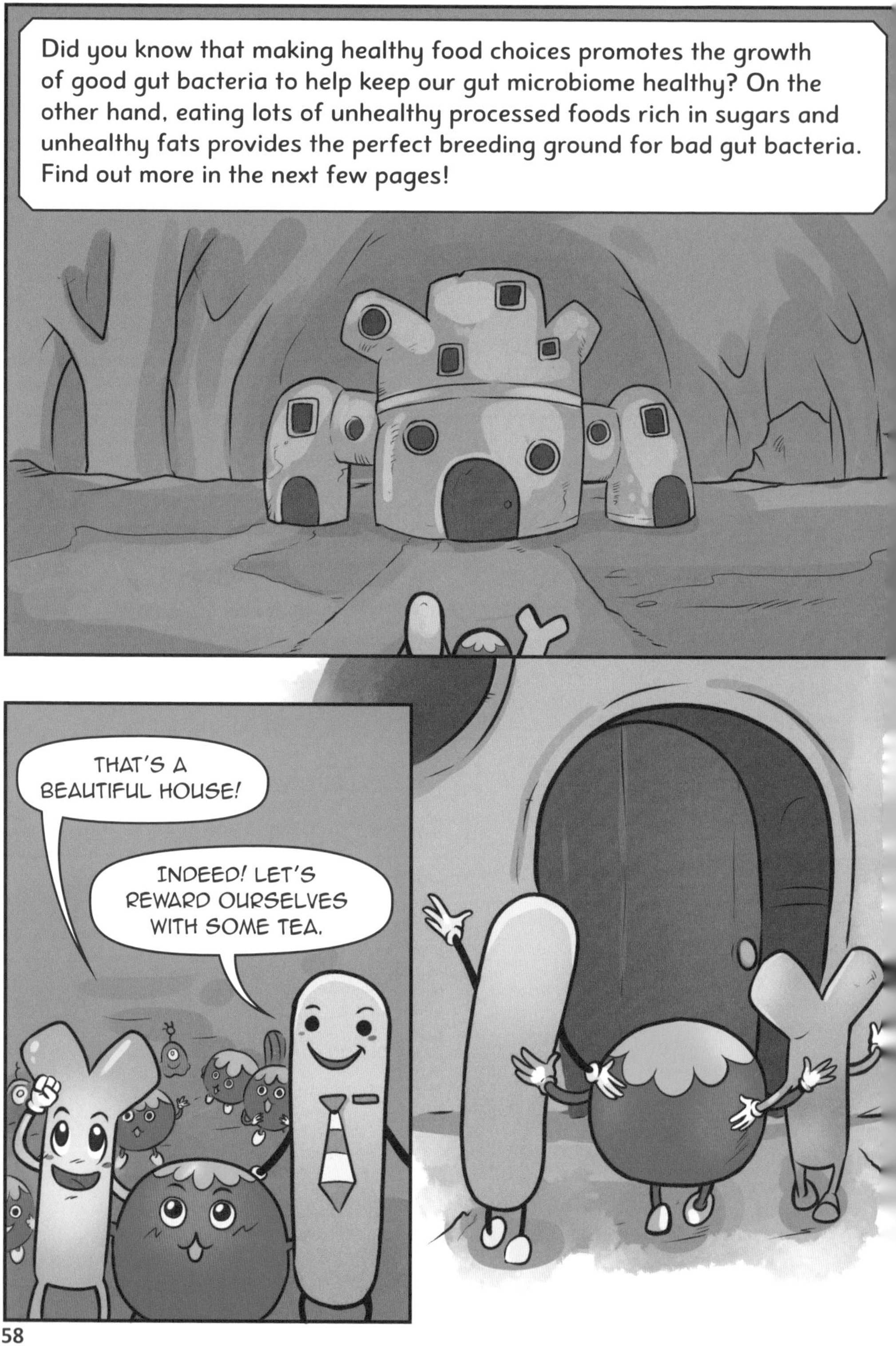
Did you know that making healthy food choices promotes the growth of good gut bacteria to help keep our gut microbiome healthy? On the other hand, eating lots of unhealthy processed foods rich in sugars and unhealthy fats provides the perfect breeding ground for bad gut bacteria. Find out more in the next few pages!
THAT'S A BEAUTIFUL HOUSE!
INDEED! LET'S REWARD OURSELVES WITH SOME TEA.

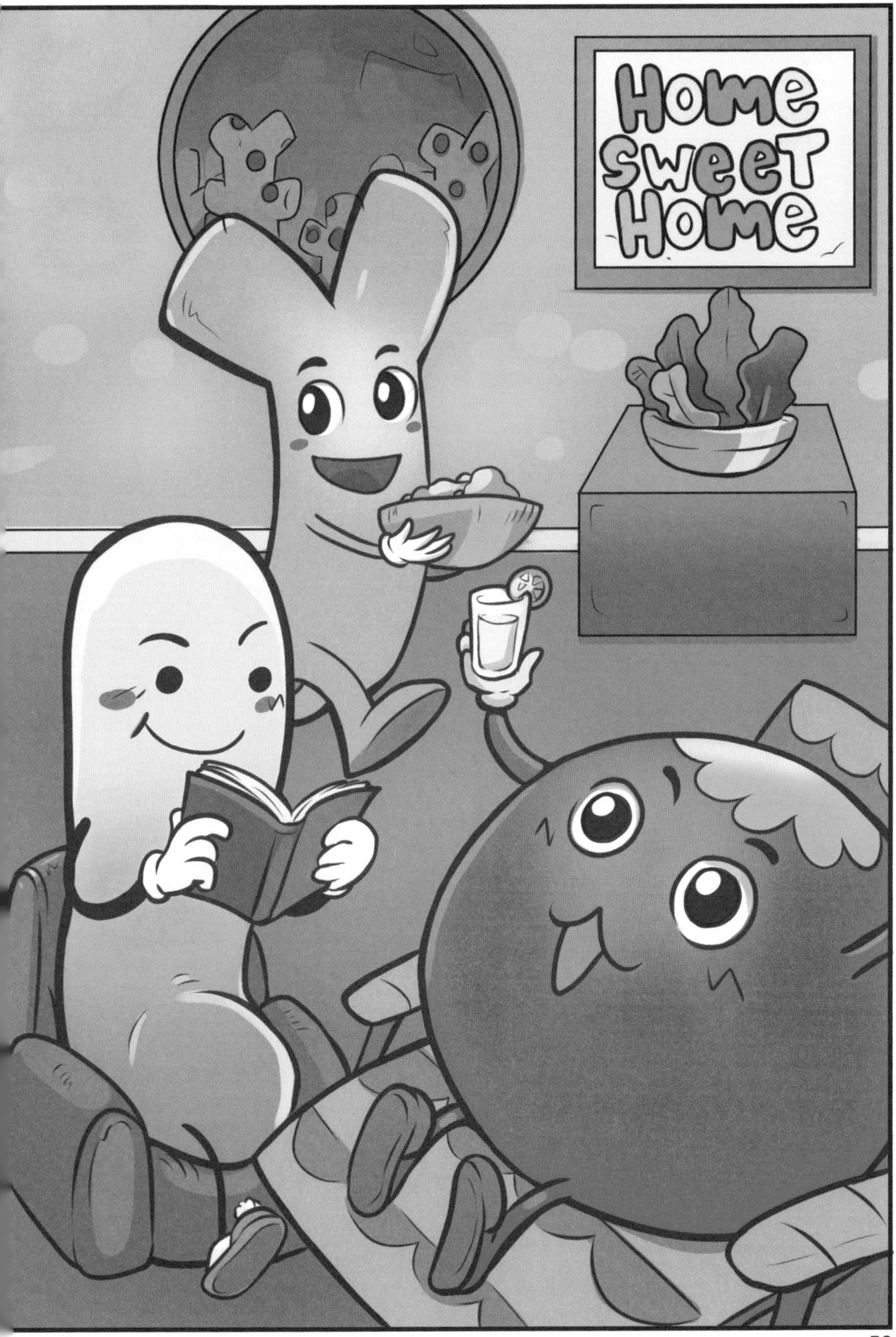
Home
Sweet
Home

More about Microbes

Microbes play essential roles in our daily lives beyond keeping us healthy. Here are some ways in which they are useful!

Marine microbes make most of the oxygen we breathe. They also absorb as much carbon dioxide as plants on land. Photosynthetic *Procholoroccus* marine bacteria account for up to 5% of the oxygen on Earth.

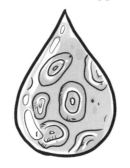

Soil microbes help convert nitrogen gas (in the atmosphere) into soil nutrients for plants to grow.

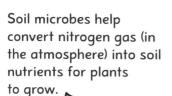

Some microbes can break down methane gas, helping to slow down global warming.

Microbes help convert food waste into fuel, providing sustainable opportunities for a circular economy.

Up to a third of the food we consume is produced by microbes. Good microbes can help extend the shelf life of foods.

Gut Microbiome and Healthy Eating

The microbes in our gut contribute to appetite regulation by producing proteins that regulate satiety, or the feeling of being full. Our feelings of hunger are related to the diversity of our gut microbiota. A less diverse microbiota is generally associated with hunger, while a more diverse microbiota is associated with satiety.

Gut microbes also contribute to our food cravings by producing metabolites that carry information from the gut to the brain, telling our body whether it needs a particular kind of food.

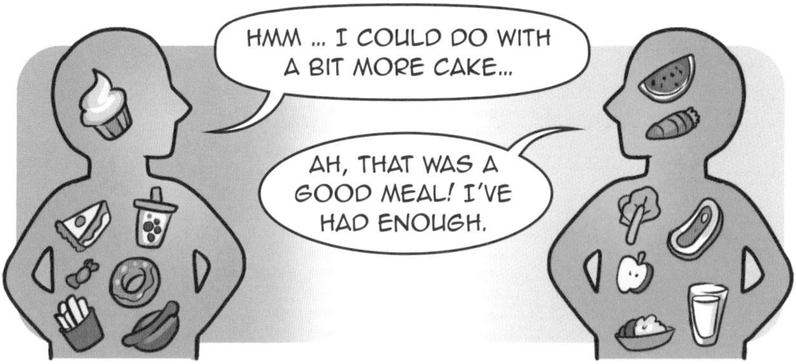
HMM ... I COULD DO WITH A BIT MORE CAKE...
AH, THAT WAS A GOOD MEAL! I'VE HAD ENOUGH.

Eating large amounts of processed foods that are high in simple sugars and fat on a regular basis promotes the growth of bad bacteria that thrive under such poor diets. These bacteria contribute to a vicious cycle of poor eating habits by further signalling to your brain their need for such foods.

Eating minimally processed whole foods promotes the diverse growth of good bacteria. These good bacteria not only produce beneficial chemicals for your health, but also signal to your brain that you are full and help you minimise unnecessary snacking.

We can help a healthy community of diverse gut microbes thrive in our gut through our food and lifestyle choices.

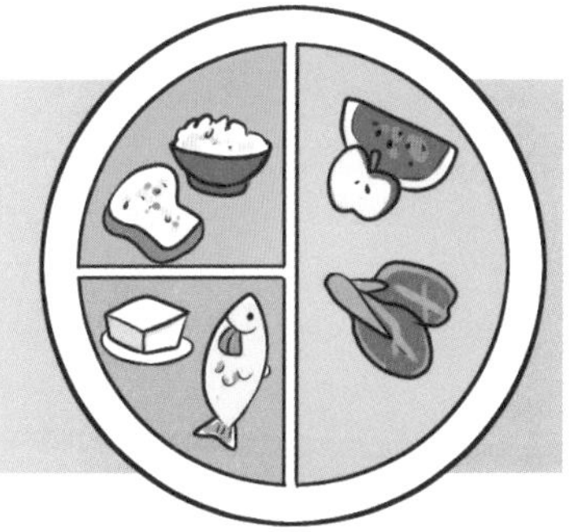

Try This Out!

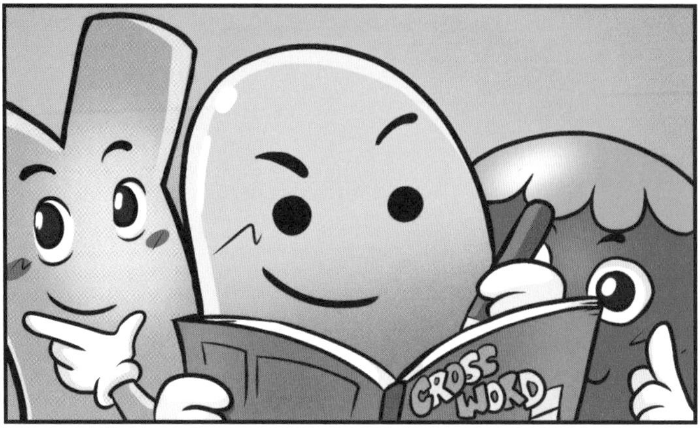
CROSS WORD

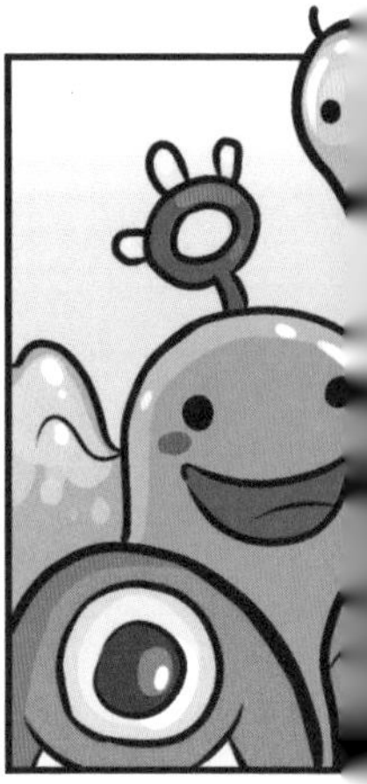

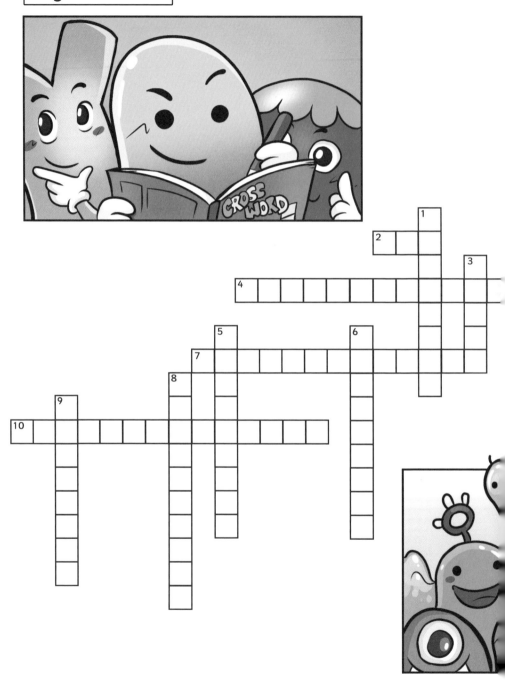

CLUES

Across

2. The store of genetic information inside living cells
4. The process whereby bacteria break down the food we eat
7. A type of asexual reproduction that bacteria use to divide into two separate identical daughter cells
10. The main site for digestion and absorption of nutrients

Down

1. Prokaryotic, single-celled organisms
3. The organ that helps the body reabsorb water
5. The process whereby our bodies break down the food that we eat
6. An illness caused by bad bacteria
8. A chemical that kills or inhibits the growth of bacteria and is used to treat bacterial infections
9. An organism that causes disease

27TH JUNE IS WORLD MICROBIOME DAY! WORLD MICROBIOME DAY CELEBRATES ALL THINGS MICROBIAL TO HIGHLIGHT THE IMPORTANCE OF MICROBES ACROSS THE WORLD.

Answers:
Across: 2. dna; 4. fermentation; 7. binary fission; 10. small intestine
Down: 1. bacteria; 3. colon; 5. digestion; 6. diarrhoea; 8. antibiotic; 9. pathogen

World of Science comics

Introducing the sensational new *World of Science* comics series designed specially for inquiring young minds! Experience Science come alive through dynamic, full-colour comics enriched by Augmented Reality.

Look out for *Tech and Gadgets, Green Movement, Germs and Your Health, Materials, More Land Animals*, and many more!

To receive updates about children's titles from WS Education, go to https://www.worldscientific.com/page/newsletter/subscribe, choose "Education", click on "Children's Books" and key in your email address.